EVANGELINE
OF THE
BAYOU

EVANGELINE
→ OF THE ←
⊹ BAYOU ⊹

by
JAN ELDREDGE

illustrations by
JOSEPH KUEFLER

Balzer + Bray
An Imprint of HarperCollins *Publishers*

Balzer + Bray is an imprint of HarperCollins Publishers.

Evangeline of the Bayou
Text copyright © 2018 by Jan Eldredge
Illustrations copyright © 2018 by Joseph Kuefler

ISBN 978-0-06-268034-1

Typography by Dana Fritts
18 19 20 21 22   CG/LSCH   10 9 8 7 6 5 4 3 2 1
❖
First Edition

For my big brother, Mark, my inspiration

—J.E.

1

They say if a sparrow taps at your window during the night, it's a sure sign death is near.

But this particular tapping wasn't meant to be a foreshadowing of Evangeline Clement's demise, at least not on this night. It was just a messenger, delivering a request from one of the bayou neighbors.

Out on the windowsill the sparrow shifted from one foot to the other, a tiny folded scrap of paper clutched in its beak. It cast an anxious glance over its shoulder, then rapped at the shack's glass pane again.

Evangeline sighed. "I'm coming. I'm coming. Keep your feathers on." Someone must have been knee-deep in desperation in order to send one of the little birds instead of a customary red cardinal. Evangeline rose from the battered wooden table, leaving her journal open and her lessons interrupted. Beneath the light of a kerosene lamp, boxes of rodent bones and jars of black nuggets lined the table-top. "If Gran had her way," she muttered, "I'd spend all my nights classifying critter carcasses and scat instead of driving out haunts."

The old cypress floorboards creaked as Evangeline strode toward the door, though the sound didn't wake Gran. She sat there in the front room alongside Evangeline, dozing in her rocking chair like she did every evening—her scarred hands folded neatly on her lap, one eye open, and snoring mightily enough to rattle the tin roof.

For a brief moment, Evangeline considered alerting her mentor to the sparrow's presence, but why disturb her night nap? After all, ghost and monster hunting flowed through her veins as surely as it flowed through Gran's, their blood running strong with the haunt huntress powers they'd inherited from their ancestors. She was more than capable of taking care of whatever job request the messenger had delivered.

Evangeline peeked out the front window at the mantle of fog crawling in from the bayou and the dark clouds drap-ing the moon. Behind the sparrow, a pair of green eyes rose from the gathering mist. Before she could even cry out, a set of fangs snapped down on the bird's tail, snatched it from the ledge, and dragged it down beneath the shroud of mist.

"No, no, no!" Evangeline leaped for the door and yanked it open. She barged across the porch and down the front steps, plunging headlong into the muggy night ringing with the racket of frog croaks and bug chirps. The lamplight emanating from inside the house did little to penetrate the murk. She clenched her teeth as well as her fists. "Let it go, Fader, you scab-crusted spawn of Satan. Drop it, or I'll get Gran. So help me, I will."

Fader shot out of the fog, his tail whipping against the leg of her jeans as he raced past her and up the front steps.

Swearing under her breath, Evangeline tore after him. She stormed into the house, slamming the door behind her. None of the commotion roused Gran, though during times of genuine distress, she was known to wake at the drop of a whisker.

With the sparrow clamped in his grinning mouth, Fader hopped onto the table and crouched in the pool of kerosene light, his tail thumping against the wood surface.

"Don't you dare kill that messenger." Evangeline narrowed her eyes at the four-eared, scruffy gray tomcat.

Fader narrowed his green eyes in return and rumbled a throaty growl. He bent back one set of ears, the second pair still jutting out the top of his head and looking for all the world like a set of small, furry devil horns.

"Fader . . . ," Evangeline warned.

The cat let his mouth drop open, and the bird plopped to the table, its tiny feet crooked and pointing upward.

"Stupid cat."

Fader lifted one of his own large paws and licked it, indifferent to Evangeline's death glare.

She scooped up the sparrow and examined it for puncture wounds. Finding none, she rubbed it against the sleeve of her camouflage T-shirt, wiping off cat spit and roughing the little creature back to consciousness. "If it were up to me, Fader, you moldy mange magnet, you'd have been gator bait years ago."

The cat yawned, unmoved, as though he knew his position as Gran's familiar would protect him from Evangeline's wrath. No one could argue he hadn't earned his keep with his daily gifts of mice, lizards, and other assorted small carcasses. *Waste not, want not,* Gran always observed. Then she would bottle the bodies, sometimes dissecting them before sorting them into containers filled with similar parts and pieces.

"Familiars," Evangeline muttered. "What are you smirking at?" She scowled at the cat. "My familiar will be showing up any day now. And you can bet it'll be far nobler than you. Probably a red fox, or maybe a broad-winged hawk." Knowing her luck, though, it'd turn out to be a crawfish or an earthworm. Her scowl melted into a frown, and stomach knotted. Whatever critter it was going to be, it'd better hurry up. She'd be turning thirteen next month, the age by which all haunt huntresses had acquired their animal familiars. And if her birthday were to come and go with still no sign of her familiar, well . . .

Well, she didn't want to think about that right now.

Within her hand the sparrow gave a shiver and opened its eyes. She set it on the tabletop, and Fader sprang over. He snatched the folded note with his teeth and jumped to the floor. He strode toward the sleeping Gran, who was still attired in her housedress and work boots, ready to leap into action if they received an urgent request, and well rested thanks to her night nap.

"Oh, no you don't!" Evangeline lunged after him, seizing him by the tail and hauling back as though yanking on the rope of a church bell. Fader let out an indignant yowl, yet managed to keep his jaws clamped.

"Mind your own beeswax." Evangeline ripped the tiny letter from his mouth, a soggy corner of it tearing away in the process. She thrust her hand toward him. "Spit out the rest of it."

Fader fixed his eyes on hers, then swallowed, taking the scrap of message to a place where she could not retrieve it.

"Fine." Evangeline pursed her lips. "I can figure it out on

my own." The sparrow fluttered up and perched on top of her head, settling comfortably into her short, dark, messy hair as she unfolded the tattered note and spread it beneath the lamplight.

The letter was addressed to Gran, with no mention of Evangeline. A cannonball of disappointment dropped into the pit of her stomach, and her face flushed.

Just because Mr. Broussard's clothesline full of laundry had been splattered with dirt and brown water the time she'd detonated that Mississippi mud man, and just because she *might* have been responsible for the collapse of Mrs. Mercier's front porch during the unfortunate galerie goblin situation, it didn't mean she wasn't capable of dealing with this new case on her own.

She tugged at her shirt collar, which suddenly felt too tight. And that incident with the hara-hand at the parish fair definitely hadn't been her fault. She'd had very little to do with the manner in which the shriveled corpse hand had ended up spinning around inside the cotton candy machine before managing to climb out and wobble its way down the midway, trailing sugary pink strings behind it. And if the fairgoers hadn't gone off on such a frantic stampede, she'd have trapped it long before that pesky raccoon shot out of nowhere and scampered away with it. The cursed hand had eventually been returned to its keeper, so no harm had been done really.

Evangeline glanced down at the note again, rereading its salutation just in case she'd somehow missed her name the first time, but it still wasn't there.

Well, it didn't matter anyway.

The sparrow danced impatiently on top of her head, but she read on, skimming through Mrs. Arseneau's hastily scrawled message and past the customary request for the services of a swamp witch. The name *swamp witch* never bothered Evangeline. It was just what the locals had always used for Gran and all their female ancestors, preferring to address them as such rather than by their official title of *haunt huntress.*

She ran her eyes farther down the page and finally reached the meat of the matter.

> . . . *such a catawampus! Gnashing and screeching and carrying on!*

A bayou banshee. Just a standard banishing. Evangeline nodded, her hope rising. This could finally be the job that proved to the council she "had heart." Then all she'd have to do was find her familiar and undergo testing of her power and talent. All her years of hard work and determination might be about to pay off.

She touched her mama's silver haunt huntress talisman hanging beneath her T-shirt, drawing reassurance from it like warmth from a sun-soaked stone. She'd have preferred to wear it outside her shirt, but it wasn't hers. To display it as such would be the equivalent of wearing a sheriff's badge when you weren't a sheriff. She allowed herself a faint grin of confidence anyway. Soon she would meet all the council's qualifications. And assuming she was of sound mind and body, they would give her a new talisman of her own. Then she'd never doubt herself again. And neither would anyone else.

She cast another glance at Mrs. Arseneau's letter. With her fingers still pressed against her mama's silver talisman, she skimmed down to the last line of the note.

There's also a . . .

But that was where the message ended. The rest of Mrs. Arseneau's words were slowly making their way through Fader's digestive tract.

The missing information could have contained anything. Hopefully it'd simply been an indication that Mrs. Arseneau would leave one of her renowned pies like she always did as barter payment for services. It'd probably be sweet potato. But a pecan pie, a flaky, buttery-crusted pecan pie, its sweet gooey inside packed with fresh meaty pecans . . . that'd be much better. Evangeline's mouth watered at the possibility.

The sparrow danced impatiently against her scalp again. She went to the front door and stuck her head out, and the tiny messenger fluttered away. Fader watched through the window, swishing his tail and licking his lips as the bird disappeared into the night.

Bypassing the crammed bookshelf, she stopped at one of the room's other towering shelves. She ran her finger along the bottles and jars crowding its ledges. *Powdered beetles, dried fish eyes, beard of goat, rusted coffin nails* . . . "Ah, there you are." She took down an old mayonnaise jar stuffed with what looked like bits of shriveled black twine. The label listed the contents as *green lizard tails*. "No shortage of these." She cast a glance at Fader, who'd curled up on the fireplace hearth. "I guess you're not *completely* useless." She withdrew a dried tail, kicked off her right boot, and dropped the appendage in, to ensure a good hunt. She pulled her boot back on and slipped a blue beaded bracelet onto her wrist for good luck.

She hurried around the room, pulling more odds and ends from cabinets and drawers, packing the tools of her trade into her leather satchel: silver handbells, juniper twigs, bottle of holy water, sack of salt, old iron key, crust of stale bread. She strapped her bowie knife onto her left thigh and donned

Gran's red hooded cloak. Her own red cloak, and even her red hoodie jacket, was buried deep in a pile of dirty clothes.

On the table she left a quick note for Gran, just as Gran often did for her. She was always posting reminders like: *Evangeline, place this goat's horn under your pillow for a good night's sleep.* Or: *Here's a vial of bullfrog urine you can apply to that wart on your elbow.* And it was just this morning she had found a note taped to the bathroom mirror advising her there was a cow dung poultice in the icebox that would knock out the headache she'd been plagued with for a week.

Evangeline took a lit lantern from its hook on the wall, stepped outside, and drew a protection pattern in chalk on one of the porch's wide wooden planks, an extra safety measure for Gran. The precaution was probably unnecessary, considering all the holly and horseshoes hanging inside the house, as well as the pair of scissors tucked beneath the doormat, but better to be overprepared than under. Gran had made more than a few supernatural enemies throughout the years. Antagonizing evil was a risk that came with the job, a risk their haunt huntress ancestors before them had also faced.

She set off down the dirt path, making her way past mossy oaks, sharp-bladed palmettos, and thick green vines. It didn't take long for the darkness and fog to swallow her up. All around, the swamp sang with sounds of life:

chirpings and skitterings, fluttering wings and snapping twigs. As she neared St. Petite's Church, the lantern's glow barely lit the trail three feet in front of her, but her eyes were sharp. "What's this?"

Lifting the light, she leaned forward. A tuft of coarse black hair clung to the bark of an old oak. Wild boar? She pulled the clump free and rubbed it between her fingers. Maybe dog? She gave it a sniff. No. Close, very close . . . but not quite dog.

She took an empty vial from her satchel and dropped the hairs inside it. She and Gran could identify them later. Whatever critter the sample had come from, it didn't matter. It'd no doubt turn out to be useful.

She trudged a few yards forward, slowing as she passed the churchyard where her mama lay buried. She gave a respectful nod. The sinkhole of sadness began to open inside her, the one that always appeared when she had thoughts of the mama she'd never known. She quickly covered it over. It wouldn't do to dwell on her loss, or the manner in which her mama's life had been violently snatched away. She had a job to do.

She stopped in her tracks again.

Something was there, watching her from among the jumble of mossy and mold-stained tombstones. A bolt of fear struck, raising the hairs on her arms and sending a surge of adrenaline coursing through her veins. Her hand went to her bowie knife at her leg, but the mist and the dark had gathered too thick for even her keen eyes to see through.

No time to be getting a case of the heebie-jeebies. It could be any one of the numerous unnatural creatures Louisiana seemed to be teeming with, many of them having arrived as stowaways. Over the years, they'd hitched rides with unsuspecting immigrants from around the world, settling and adapting to their new southern environment as seamlessly as the humans had. And while not all of them were malevolent, Louisiana certainly had more than its fair share of hostile ghosts, monsters, and other assorted supernatural nasties.

She rubbed down the goose bumps. Well, as long as whatever it was stayed where it was and didn't cause her any trouble, it wasn't her business. She moved on, the weight of the creature's gaze clinging to her back like marshy sludge. It definitely wasn't human. That was for sure. She hurried her steps, the rushing of her feet keeping time with the rushing of her heart.

The farther Evangeline traveled from the bayou's slow-moving waters, the more the fog thinned and the path cleared. She tried to focus on the job waiting ahead, but her mind kept skipping back to the thing in the graveyard. She sifted through a litany of Gran's lessons on supernatural beings.

The creature might have been nothing more than a creeper, that pesky species of specter known for taking the form of a cypress tree knee and waiting motionless until an evening passerby happened along. As soon as its target was in range, it'd rise up and float silently after them. Creepy, but harmless. And easily dissipated with the swipe of a lantern: the light would slice it in two and send its remains fluttering to the ground like a pair of dead leaves.

Or, maybe it'd been a Johnny revenant, the reanimated, moldering corpse of a Civil War soldier. She really hated those things, galumphing through the swamps, their shrill rebel yells announcing their arrival. Of course, they'd all been disarmed long ago by her haunt huntress ancestors, but that didn't deter the creatures from swooping up broken tree limbs and brandishing them like sabers, giving you a sound wallop to the head if you weren't quick enough to clear out of their path. They only came out after a big rain, though, when storm-torn branches were strewn aplenty, and the weather of late had been dry.

She'd thought of at least half a dozen other possibilities by the time she arrived at the Arseneaus' old two-story cypress-plank home, but none of the options matched up with her gut feeling. Gran was a true believer in listening to your instincts. "Trust your gut, Evangeline," she was always saying. "It sees what the eyes don't."

As Evangeline set down her lantern, a barred owl hooted from the rooftop. An omen of bad luck if she'd ever heard one. She cursed beneath her breath.

The owl *hoo-hooo*ed again in its lonely, mournful way. It stared down at her with eyes as round and black as the empty eye sockets of a ghost.

Frowning and tapping the tips of her fingers together, she assessed the situation as Gran had taught her. Laundry on the line. Toys in the yard. The family must have evacuated quickly, probably staying in Thibodaux with Mrs. Arseneau's sister.

From the side of the house a low moan rose, building to a tormented wail.

"I hear you. I hear you," Evangeline murmured. She pulled off Gran's red cloak, folded it, and set it aside. She dug through the satchel strapped across her chest and took out the crust of bread, followed by the sack of salt, which she dumped into her hand. She spat on the ground for added protection, then straightened her shoulders and fixed her eyes on the side of the house. Steadying her voice, careful to make it clear and confident, she called out, "What is it you seek?"

The wailing abruptly ceased, and the banshee floated into the front yard. Clad in a shapeless, drab-gray dress, the ghostly being hovered and bobbed in midair, peering upon Evangeline with anguished eyes. It peeled back its cracked lips and gave her a silent snarl.

Evangeline took a deep breath, quickly reviewing what she knew about bayou banshees. They almost always came from the cemetery at the ladies' state penitentiary thirty miles up the road. These weren't the restless ghosts of petty criminals; these spirits were the truly rotten ones, murderers of the innocent. They'd died behind bars, sometimes from illness, but mostly through injury. A few of them had been launched into the afterlife with the aid of Gruesome Gertie, Louisiana's electric chair. Either way, their stained souls clung to this world, not wanting to face the consequences of their deeds, the consequences awaiting them on the other side.

While some people held the belief that every soul was met with forgiveness at the end of the road, Evangeline didn't think so. She'd dealt with enough reluctant otherworldly beings to suspect that cruelty and viciousness on this side of life were not looked upon lightly on the other side.

The banshee whipped its head back. It let out a shriek, shattering a window at the rear of the house and sending glass tinkling to the ground. The desolate spirit gnashed its teeth and snatched at its wispy hair that wavered like cobweb strands in the wind. Up on the roof, the barred owl gave a startled hoot and flapped silently away.

Evangeline thrust the crust of bread and the palm full of salt toward the ghost. "Return to your place of rest, and wander from there no more."

The banshee didn't retreat. Evangeline hadn't really expected it to. Though salt and bread were known to drive away evil spirits by absorbing their psychic energy, she found the two ingredients hardly ever worked. But Gran always insisted they be the first attempt, since both were cheap and plentiful.

The banshee turned away and flew onto the front porch. It swooped from one end to the other as though caught up in a powerful psychic current. It shrieked again, and the sound of breaking glass followed.

"Dang it!" Mrs. Arseneau would return fit to be tied if all her windows got shattered. Evangeline tossed the salt to one side and the bread to the other. A raccoon shot out of the bushes, snatched up the stale crust, and skittered away into the night.

Evangeline pulled a juniper twig and a silver bell from her satchel. She lit the stick and waved it with one hand while ringing the bell with her other. The piney-pungent odor and sharp jangling drifted through the heavy night air. She recited a quick incantation and again demanded the restless ghost return to its grave or cross to the other side.

Her efforts were met with another screech and another shattered window.

"Fine." Evangeline set her jaw. "Let's try something a bit more powerful, then." She dropped the bell and twig and brought out the bottle of holy water from her stash of supplies.

The banshee froze, stopping in midwail. Its gaunt face twisted into an expression of terror. It rocketed off the porch

and straight toward Evangeline, its spirit force plowing her down and nearly knocking her out of her priest-blessed, silver-tipped, alligator-skin boots.

The impact with the ground shot through Evangeline's tailbone and raced up her spine, sending her eyes rolling back. "Blast it!" she rasped, climbing to her feet. But the banshee was gone, its wails trailing after it like smoke from an extinguished candle.

Evangeline returned the potent holy water to her satchel, brushed the dirt off the back of her jeans as best she could, then assessed the situation. A few broken windows, but overall, a job well done, the work of a bona fide haunt huntress. Even if that haunt huntress' name hadn't been included on the job request. She went to retrieve the juniper twig and silver bell and paused.

Something had drawn up behind her, its steady breaths rattling deep inside it.

Goose bumps skipped across her arms and raced down the back of her spine. Not wanting to, but not able to stop herself, she peered into one of the house's unbroken front windows. A pair of yellow eyes reflected off the dark glass, yellow eyes staring out from the hairy black face of a four-legged beast standing no more than three yards behind her.

She didn't know what the creature was, and she didn't wait around to figure it out. She snatched her lantern and hightailed it up the steps and into the hundred-year-old house built by Mr. Arseneau's great-great-granddaddy. She slammed the door behind her, sending it wobbling on its rain-rusted hinges. Heart booming, she scrabbled around the inside of her satchel, found the stick of chalk, and scratched a series of protection symbols onto the door's wood panel.

Outside, the front steps creaked. The porch boards groaned as thick claws clicked across them. The being stopped and dragged its nails along the other side of the rickety old door, surely leaving a row of gouges trailing down the surface.

At that moment Evangeline realized two things. Firstly, it was this yellow-eyed, hairy black creature, and not her use of the holy water, that had driven the banshee away. And secondly, this same creature was the one that had watched her from the graveyard. There was no doubt in her mind about this. She felt it in her gut.

She eyeballed her hastily sketched chalk symbols, then stepped back with a satisfied nod.

Out on the porch the creature raked its claws down the other side of the door again, but she wasn't worried. "Go ahead and scratch all you want. Whatever you are." Evangeline couldn't help but smirk. "My chalk protection will hold against an evil being like you." She sniffed the air, and her heart lifted even more. Was that pie? She raised her lantern and peered toward the kitchen. Yes. Yes, it was. And there it sat, right on the counter. *Pecan* instead of sweet potato, after all.

The thing clawed the door again. "You're wasting your time, night creature!" She broke into a fully loaded grin. "I can wait here as long as it takes. Come daybreak, you'll flee the sun's rays and slink back to the shadows, just like your kind always do."

In the kitchen across the room, the raccoon shimmied through the small window's broken pane. With Evangeline's stale piece of offering-bread still clutched in its mouth, it hopped down onto the counter. It waddled over to the pie, lowered its black nose to the syrupy sweet pecans, and sniffed.

"You get away from that! Shoo!" Evangeline stomped her boot.

The raccoon tossed the hard hunk of bread over its shoulder, sat up, and plunged both black paws through the center of the pie.

"Hey! That's mine, you thieving vermin!" She dashed over as it scooped up two handfuls of gooey, nutty filling and shoved them into its mouth. Flaky, buttery crust crumbs rained down; a lone syrupy pecan plopped to the counter. With cheeks bulging, the masked bandit scrambled out the broken window, its bushy ringed tail disappearing into the night after it.

"Dang it!" Evangeline pounded her fist against the counter.

Out on the front porch, the graveyard creature threw itself against the door, hitting it with a boom and rattling it in its frame.

Evangeline cast a worried glance over her shoulder. "It'll hold," she reassured herself.

She set the lantern down and whipped her knife from the sheath on her leg, determined to cut away a small portion of pie the raccoon hadn't defiled. She sank the blade into the nutty topping and had set about carving an irregular-shaped wedge when the thing outside threw itself at the door again, and this time the frame gave a loud crack.

Evangeline whirled around. One of the door's rusty hinges popped off and clunked across the hardwood floor.

Muttering a curse, she grabbed her lantern and bolted away, down the short dark hallway and into Mr. and Mrs. Arseneau's bedroom. She threw the door shut and twisted the lock.

From the front of the house came the sound of the door bursting inward and banging into the wall.

Evangeline turned and lifted the lantern, assessing her situation by the murky golden light.

In one corner sat the bed covered with Mrs. Arseneau's hand-sewn patchwork quilt; her hand-sewn flowery-print curtains framed the room's only window. Next to the huge fireplace rested a stack of wooden crates filled with Mr. Arseneau's medicinal homemade root beer. Evangeline grimaced at the sight of them. She'd recently had the misfortune of sampling one of the sickly sweet noncarbonated drinks, and found it tasted nothing like the frosty cold bottles of Barq's you could buy at Pichon's General Store.

Out in the hallway, claws clicked slowly toward the bedroom and stopped outside it. A sniffing sounded between the door and its frame.

Evangeline rushed to the window and gave it an upward heave, but it didn't budge. She gripped tighter and tried again, grunting with effort, but it had been sealed shut sash to sill by a hundred years' worth of paint.

She was trapped good.

She backed away, praying these door hinges were stronger than the others. She bumped into the bed behind her, and a pale, long-fingered hand shot out from underneath. It grasped her booted ankle and yanked her foot out from under her.

Evangeline's lantern went flying, and she crashed to the floor, her face smacking against the hard cypress planks as the lantern shattered.

3

A kerosene-fueled flame whooshed onto one of Mrs. Arseneau's home-sewn curtains, licking its way up the flowery-print fabric as greedily as a raccoon gobbling pecan pie.

Before Evangeline could scramble even halfway to her feet, a second pale hand shot out and clutched her other ankle, sinking its claws deep enough to carve marks in the hide of her gator-skin boots.

"You're gonna ruin my boots, blast you!"

The beast outside the bedroom door snarled.

The thing under the bed reeled her in. As it dragged her toward the darkness surrounding it, the last lines of Mrs. Arseneau's message came back to her: *There's also a . . .*

"Dag blam it!" Mrs. Arseneau hadn't been talking about a payment-for-services pie. She meant they had a shadow croucher under their bed. Evangeline reached for her knife, but her hand brushed only an empty sheath. "Dag blam it again!" Her knife was in the kitchen, sticking out of the pecan pie.

Fingers of icy panic snatched at her heart, but there was no way she was going to let them grab ahold. She reminded herself of Gran's words on the subject: *Fear is a steel trap. It keeps you from moving forward. It binds up your courage as well as your smarts.*

Evangeline took a deep breath and forced her anxiety down—a feat that sometimes proved to be as easy as shoving a pillow into a matchbox.

Gritting her teeth, she gave a hard yank and wrenched a foot free. She kicked the shadow croucher in its face, the silver tip of her boot impacting with a sizzle and singe.

The monster screeched and let go of her other ankle.

Evangeline pawed her way out from under the bed, scrambling across the floor like a daddy longlegs skating on water. As she glanced behind instead of ahead, her palm landed on a shard of lantern glass. Flesh split. Kerosene rushed into the wound, spreading like wildfire through a marsh. Wincing and cursing, she pulled the shard away. She balled her wounded hand into a fist and moved forward, doing her best not to leave bloody handprints in her wake. In the process, she crawled through a puddle of kerosene, soaking both knees of her jeans.

The fire devouring Mrs. Arseneau's curtains crackled, sending out rolls of dark smoke. Evangeline coughed, and her eyes watered. The heat warmed her face.

The beast in the hallway gave a long howl and threw itself at the door with a loud *whomp*.

Evangeline peered under the bed. The glow from the flaming curtains cast just enough light for her to make out the shadow croucher's features. A figure the size of a large child stared back at her through beady black eyes set in a ghostly-white snouted face. It hunkered on black hairy arms and legs beneath a hairy gray torso. A long, scaly tail lay curled alongside it like a pink snake. It opened its pale mouth wide, bared its needle-sharp fangs, and hissed.

"Hush your face!" Evangeline's injured hand throbbed miserably, and her eyes stung from the smoke. She was in no mood for attitude, especially from a creature that had been stupid enough to feed from the tree of fear. "You're the one who got yourself into this mess. You know better than to eat that poisonous fruit. And now look at you, grown just as large and out of control as fear itself."

Gran's words rose to mind again. *Fear is a powerful poison. It turns peaceful beings into monsters, beasts that will strike*

first without even thinking.

"I would've expected such behavior from a gluttonous raccoon," Evangeline continued, "but I always thought possums had more sense."

The monster that had once been a standard-size possum snapped its pink tail and hissed again.

Evangeline sighed wearily. She could nag all day, but it wouldn't get the shadow croucher out from under the bed. And she sure couldn't drag it out, not without getting mauled in the process. Nor could she leave it there to claw at ankles and gnaw on toes in the night. Some shadow crouchers had been known to bite the toes right off any foot they found dangling.

Adding to her growing list of challenges was the problem of what to do with the monster once she did manage to get it out from under the bed. If only she'd packed a bottle of Gran's taming tincture in her satchel, she could easily have calmed the creature right there where it hunkered, triggering the process that would slowly return it to its normal size and disposition.

The beast in the hallway threw itself at the door again.

The air was growing thicker with black smoke. She coughed and waved her hand in front of her. The fire would soon jump from the drapes, hit the spilled kerosene, and race through the room.

She tried to focus. A real haunt huntress would know what to do. And she *was* a haunt huntress. Just not yet officially.

She thought for a moment.

The first order of business was getting the fire put out. That much was clear. Another Gran-ism came to her. *Improvise. Use what you know, and use what you've got.*

Evangeline fumbled around inside her nearly empty satchel, past the stick of chalk, the box of matches, and the vial containing the tuft of black hair she'd picked off the oak tree. Her fingers closed around the bottle of holy water. It wasn't nearly enough to douse the flames. She needed a plan.

She glanced around the room, and her eyes settled on the crates of Mr. Arseneau's medicinal root beer.

She found her plan.

As soon as she could get the fire doused, she'd deal with the monster under the bed. Then she'd face down the

the hallway. She had her work cut out for her.
r sure. She'd be busier than a cat covering scat
floor.

The graveyard beast uttered a desolate wail and clawed at the door.

Evangeline cast an uneasy glance in its direction. Eventually, it would scratch its way clean through. But she couldn't worry about that right now. She climbed to her feet and rushed toward the stash of root beer. She pulled down a crate, popped open the ceramic swing-top caps, and lugged the case to the window.

Pouring and sloshing bottle after bottle onto the flames, she extinguished the curtains, quickly reducing them to a set of soggy, steaming rags.

The odor of smoke, kerosene, and sugary-sweet root beer saturated the air. At least she'd managed to put out the fire, but she'd also put out the room's only source of light.

Shuffling and hissing, and driven by fear, the shadow croucher dragged itself out from under the bed. By now it would know enough to avoid her silver toe tips. This time when it attacked, no doubt it'd make sure to do so above her boots.

Her heart was thumping hard enough to quiver her eyeballs. She focused her thoughts, narrowing in on a solution to the problem creeping across the floor toward her.

If she could trap it, bundle it up in a blanket, she could bring it home. Then she and Gran could calm it and release it back into the swamp. It wasn't much of a plan, but she had to try. She certainly couldn't leave it in its current form, free to go on a toe-mauling rampage.

The shadow croucher hissed, its claws ticking against the cypress floorboards as it crawled closer.

Evangeline backed away, fumbling through her satchel.

The beast outside the door snarled low and deep and menacing.

She pulled out her matches and struck one. The tiny flame shed enough illumination to guide her to the fireplace and the kerosene lamp perched on its mantel.

The creature in the hallway threw itself at the door. The frame shuddered; it wouldn't hold much longer.

Evangeline lit the lamp's wick, and it blazed into a small golden light.

The shadow croucher drew back, hissing and shielding its face with its long-fingered hands.

"Now, you just sit right there and don't move." Keeping her eyes on the shadow croucher, Evangeline began to ease Mrs. Arseneau's handmade quilt from the bed.

The monster shot past her. It dove into the fireplace and scrambled up the brick walls of the chimney.

"No!" She ripped the quilt away and lunged after the

creature, throwing the blanket and her arms around its back end.

It struggled and hissed. One of its rear legs popped free from her grasp, striking her face and slicing a gash down her left cheek. If there was pain, she didn't notice it. The shadow croucher wiggled the rest of the way free and clambered up the chimney. It escaped onto the roof, down to the yard, and into the night.

Evangeline cursed. She rushed to the window, pushed the root beer–drenched tatters aside, and peered out.

Beneath the moonlight, the shadow croucher scuttled away on all fours, gnashing its teeth and swishing its snaky pink tail behind it. It disappeared into the nearby trees and foliage.

Scowling, Evangeline rapped her knuckles against the window pane. "You can't get away from Evangeline Clement! I'm not finished with you! I am a haunt huntress! And don't you forget it!"

From out in the hallway came the sound of the hairy, yellow-eyed graveyard creature scrambling away, its claws clicking and clacking and fading as it retreated out the front door and down the porch steps.

Evangeline stood silent for a moment. Then she stepped over to the door, pressed her ear against it, and listened carefully, but there was no sound of the big creature's return.

It must have decided the shadow croucher was an easier meal to catch. And that meant she wouldn't have to worry about capturing and calming it anymore. "Poor little thing." She sighed. But that was the way of the swamp. One critter always eating another.

She took the kerosene lamp from the mantel and eased the bedroom door open. She peered into the dark hallway. Still nothing. She hurried out to the kitchen, found a piece of paper and a pencil nub, and left a quick note for Mrs. Arseneau:

The banshee has been banished, and the shadow croucher is gone. Unfortunately, a raccoon ate the pecan pie, but that's okay. There won't be any charge for my services.
Evangeline Clement

She thought of adding an offer to sew a new set of bedroom curtains, but recalling her previous failed attempts with a needle and thread, she decided a pair of store-bought window coverings might be more appreciated instead.

No longer hungry, she pulled her knife from the pie and wiped its blade on the leg of her kerosene-soaked, soot-stained jeans. Outside, she retrieved the bell and juniper stick and donned Gran's red cloak. Then she set off for home.

As she trudged down the path, something rustled through the palmettos and wild azaleas alongside her. It might have been nothing more than that six-legged hydrangean lizard she'd seen frequenting the area, but she didn't stop to investigate. She picked up her pace and hurried onward.

Evangeline reached home in the predawn hour, aching, and reeking of smoke and kerosene and sweet, sticky root beer. She climbed the porch steps and dragged herself inside, where she hung Gran's red cloak on the hook. Gran had retired from the front room rocking chair. Her snores drifted out from her bedroom down the hall.

In the tiny bathroom, Evangeline tended to her wounds. As she drew the tin of calendula salve from the medicine cabinet, she caught sight of her reflection in the age-spotted mirror. Her eye was blackening to a purple-plum color, and an angry red scratch from the shadow croucher's back claw ran down her cheek. A jagged gash from the broken lantern lay across her palm. She looked like she'd been on the losing end of a catfight with a cougar. She felt like it too.

She applied the greasy salve to her cuts and bandaged her hand, then cast a glance at the claw-footed tub. But she was far too tired to take a bath, even though she desperately needed one.

In her bedroom, she removed her satchel and gator-skin boots. She rummaged around in the pile of dirty clothes on the floor, pulled out a T-shirt, and used it to wipe down her boots, frowning at the gouges left by the shadow croucher. Those boots had been her first barter payment, and she'd worked hard to earn them, assisting Gran with the eviction of a tizzy of blood faes from Old Man LeBlanc's tannery shed. Unfortunately, the other half of that job payment had involved a barbeque lunch of undercooked venison, the outside blackened crispy, the inside bright bloody pink. Evangeline didn't consider herself to be a picky eater, but there were a few foods she simply couldn't abide. Undercooked meat was one of them.

She fell onto the bed, still dressed in her soot-stained jeans and camouflage T-shirt, right on top of the faded patchwork quilt that'd been the first barter payment Gran had earned, back when Gran was a fresh new haunt huntress, her youthful skin still smooth and unscarred.

Gran was just about her age when she'd earned the quilt all on her own, though Gran had long since had her familiar by then. Not that it mattered. It wasn't a race. She'd find her familiar soon, and she'd prove she had heart.

The combination of those two things would ignite a strong magic inside her. Her new powers, combined with the skills she'd been learning all her life, would make her a haunt huntress just as talented as her mama and Gran.

But what if those things don't happen? a slithery voice murmured from the back of her mind. *What if your thirteenth birthday comes and goes with no sign of your familiar, and with not even a spark of your powers emerging? What if you're nothing more than a . . .*

"No!" Her whispered denial burst out with such force, she half expected it to wake the snoring Gran across the hall. A rock-hard lump swelled in her throat.

No. She was not a *middling.* She was a haunt huntress—descended from a long, proud line of haunt huntresses. Her mama had passed the basic powers along to her just as all their female ancestors had done for more than two hundred years, genetically handing those powers down from each mama to her only child, always a girl child. She was not the end to Gran's line. She was not one of those rare and random descendants born without any magical abilities. She was sure of it. She squeezed her eyes shut, willing sleep to fall over her, knowing full well the dark doubt would return tomorrow, clawing to be let back in.

Eventually, consciousness slipped away like muddy water through her fingers, and sleep overcame her.

It seemed like she'd dozed for only a few minutes before she awakened to the sounds of Gran clattering around in the kitchen. The aroma of strong coffee drifted into her bedroom. Her stomach growled irritably, but her exhaustion was more powerful.

She dropped back into wonderful, deep, dark sleep.

Something scratched at her windowpane, making a frantic *squeak-squeak-squeaking*. A desperate yowling joined the desperate scraping.

"Fader . . . ," Evangeline grumbled. She pulled the pillow over her head, but it did no good. The cat's yowls penetrated the feather-filled barrier like arrows through her eardrums.

Tossing the pillow aside, Evangeline sat up, her eyelids as heavy as Gran's cast-iron gumbo pots. "Stupid cat." She stumbled out of bed and raised the window, and Fader shot in. He scampered through her bedroom and out to the kitchen.

She plopped back into bed, just drifting toward sleep again when Gran rapped the silver handle of her ash-wood cane against the doorframe. "Evangeline!" She stuck her gray-haired head into the room. "We're needed."

"Want sleep," Evangeline muttered.

"Coffee's getting cold." Gran left, her cane tap-tapping as she hobbled up the hallway.

Evangeline groaned.

"And for the love of Lilith," Gran called out, "wash up. You smell like a polecat that's been steeped in sewer water."

Yawning, Evangeline dragged herself upright. Her knee itched something fierce, and she scratched it, a sure sign she'd soon be kneeling inside a strange church. Not a welcoming omen. Churches she loved. Unfamiliar places, not so much.

"Evangeline Clement!" Gran called,

Her words would have carried more weight if Evangeline's middle name had been included in the command. But she didn't have a middle name. She was just Evangeline Clement.

"Get your carcass moving. We're needed."

"Yes, ma'am." With a groan, Evangeline swung her feet over the side of the bed. "We're needed," she reminded herself, the two words as commanding to a haunt huntress as a fire alarm to a fireman. Yawning and scratching her knee again, she tottered out to the bathroom.

Freshly bathed and no longer reeking like a skunk dunked in a cesspool, Evangeline took a seat at the table. The dreamy aroma of egg bread floated over from one of Gran's skillets. Sausages sizzled in the pan beside it. She inhaled deeply, and her stomach rumbled expectantly.

Gran set a full plate before her, then returned and plunked a steaming mug alongside it. She took in Evangeline's black eye, wounded cheek, and bandaged hand. She raised a gray eyebrow but asked no questions.

Evangeline provided no answers. She grasped the mug with both hands and drank. The strong coffee and chicory coursed through her veins like magic. The world came into focus, drawing her one step closer to consciousness, one step closer to tackling whatever new case they were needed for. She tore into a slice of egg bread, barely giving it a chew before swallowing. A night of haunt hunting always left her famished.

"Slow down." Gran frowned. The faded scar running down the side of her face seemed to frown with her. "Dignity. Self-control. Those are the traits of a haunt huntress. Not gobbling and snuffling like a wild boar."

"Yes, ma'am," Evangeline murmured around a mouthful of egg bread. She swallowed, then cleared her throat. "The Arseneaus had a banshee problem last night, but I took care of it, along with the shadow croucher under their bed."

Gran fixed her eyes on Evangeline. "Did you leave the surroundings as you found them?"

Evangeline took a huge bite of egg bread, and then another, her cheeks puffing like a nutria with a maw full of marsh roots. It was bad manners to speak with your mouth full.

Gran's expression hardened. "Evangeline . . ."

Evangeline chewed, then reluctantly gulped down the clump of egg bread. "Well, it's not like I burned the *entire* house down."

Gran closed her eyes, murmuring a self-reminder that she'd have to smooth things over with Mrs. Arseneau.

Before Gran could ask for more details, Evangeline jumped up and raced off to retrieve the sample of black hair she'd collected from the oak tree.

"I found this last night." She offered the vial to Gran and sat back down to her breakfast.

Gran took the top off the vial and sniffed the contents. She pursed her lips. "Where'd you get this?"

"Near St. Petite's graveyard."

"Oh." Gran nodded as though Evangeline's answer some- how explained everything. She placed the vial on one of the shelves and went back to her chores. "Finish up. We have a case to prepare for." She plunged the skillet into the sink, her strong arms disappearing up to her elbows in sudsy water.

"So, who's the job for?" Evangeline asked, taking another bite.

Gran gave the pan a good scrubbing, then ran it under a cool stream of water. "A family in New Orleans."

Evangeline stopped in midchew, her appetite shriveling like a frog carcass on a sun-baked highway. "New Orleans? Why us?"

"They're without a haunt huntress." Gran paused for a moment, her shoulders drooping ever so slightly. She took a deep breath and cleared her throat before continuing. "And until her daughter grows to age, we all take our turns helping out when needed."

Evangeline didn't want to be insensitive to the plight of the young and motherless New Orleanian haunt huntress. Her own mama's absence still left her with a gaping emptiness, even though she'd been too young to know her before she'd been killed in the line of haunt huntress duty. Evangeline swallowed the lump in her throat. "Can't someone else do it?"

"Finish up," Gran repeated. "We have a lot of preparations to make before Percy fetches us this afternoon."

Gran had spoken. And that was that.

Evangeline turned her mouth down and pushed her plate away. The city was noisy and crowded, with too many people and too many tall buildings. And it smelled funny. She didn't feel comfortable in cities, and she most definitely didn't feel comfortable around city folk with their fancy cars and their fancy sense of style. She'd much rather stay here in the swamp, where things made more sense and where life abided by a peaceful order and hierarchy.

"Stop pouting," Gran said as she wiped the pan dry with a dish towel. She didn't have to look at Evangeline to read her expression.

"Yes, ma'am."

As Evangeline carried her empty plate and mug to the sink, Gran tossed a leftover sausage link to Fader, but he stayed hunkered beneath the table, his tail tucked between his legs and pouting as severely as Evangeline. Normally he'd be weaving between Gran's feet, yowling up at her for a morsel of meat. It was a wonder Gran never tripped over the stupid cat.

In a flash of gray, an ankle-high yimmby shot out from under a kitchen cabinet. It dashed across the floor on its two stick legs, its little potbelly bouncing, the wiry white hairs on its round head swaying like a tuft of weeds in a breeze. It seized the sausage out from under Fader's nose and then ran its saucer-round gaze about the room, mapping the quickest route of escape.

Evangeline dove beneath the table, grasped the yimmby by its skinny leg, and yanked it off its feet. The sausage flew from its clutch and rolled to a stop back beneath Fader's nose.

Gripping its ankle between her forefinger and thumb, she carried the squirming creature to the front door and threw it out. She and Gran never minded sharing food with a hungry critter in need, but a yimmby would eat you out of house and home if not kept in check.

The yimmby jumped to its long feet and rounded on Evangeline, uttering a high-pitched *kik-kik-kik*ing sound and shaking its little fist at her. Leaving it there to scold, Evangeline fetched the sausage, tossed it outside, and slammed the door shut.

Gran arched an eyebrow at Fader, still crouching immobile beneath the table. Then she turned and dunked Evangeline's cup and plate into the suds-filled sink and gave them a scrub.

"What's our job in New Orleans?" Evangeline asked.

Gran rinsed the dishes, set them into the drainer, and dried her hands on a towel. She crossed the room, her cane clumping against the floor. She rummaged through a large trunk and took out a beat-up brown leather valise that had witnessed many a hunt.

"Gran?" Evangeline prodded.

"Go pack your things, Evangeline." Gran went to one of the shelves and ran her finger along the bottles and jars lining it.

"Yes, ma'am." When Gran was ready, she'd tell her

more. Nonetheless, an uneasy feeling unfurled in the pit of her stomach. Gran was seldom mute on matters, and when she was, it didn't bode well.

Mumbling to herself, Gran pulled the large valise open and began filling it with a variety of pastes, powders, and ointments. Frowning and absently rubbing the silver haunt huntress talisman around her neck—always a sign she had something weighty on her heart—she moved to her bedroom to add more supplies.

Evangeline went to her own room, trying not to sulk every step of the way. Fader trotted along after her with his fur bristling. He leaped onto the window ledge and stared outside. Two of his four ears bent back, and his tail swished. He whispered a fang-baring hiss, then jumped down and scurried underneath Evangeline's bed.

"What's gotten into you, you four-eared chicken?" Evangeline peered out the window, and her heart stopped.

There among the side yard spider lilies and the muscadine grapevine, just below the tallow tree, stood a huge black dog. It waited not more than six feet away, its droopy jowls and broad snout pointing toward the house. With its massive head, thick neck, and muscular legs, it had to weigh at least two hundred pounds. The creature gazed at Evangeline through mournful yellow eyes, the same yellow eyes she'd seen reflected off the Arseneaus' front window last night.

If her boots hadn't been rooted to the floor, she would have dived under the bed with Fader.

"A grim." She could barely whisper the dreaded words. It was this beast, its shaggy fur matted with twigs and mud, that had watched her from St. Petite's graveyard last night, followed her to the Arseneaus' house, then burst open their front door in its determination to get to her. And if she wasn't mistaken, it was this very beast that had skulked unseen through the palmettos and wild azaleas alongside her as she'd made her way home. The tuft of black hair she'd found clinging to the tree near St. Petite's graveyard had no doubt come from this grim.

Her legs went weak, and she grasped the windowsill for support. The presence of a black grim could mean only one thing.

She was about to die, and it was here to escort her soul to the other side.

What else had Gran taught her about grims, besides the fact they frequented the final resting places of the dead? She searched her memory.

Sometimes they appeared at the scene of an accident. They also showed up when someone had a bad illness and would soon be passing on. But she felt perfectly fine. She cast a worried glance in the direction of Gran's room, and then she knew with a sinking certainty. The creature wasn't here for her. It had come for Gran.

She should have known. It'd been only yesterday that she'd noticed the silver tips of her boots needed polishing, a sure sign someone close was near death. She gasped as another thought hit, punching her right in the gut and nearly doubling her over. She'd been wearing Gran's red cloak last night. The grim must have mistaken her for Gran. It was only when she'd yelled out her own name to the flee-ing shadow croucher that the grim had left the house. Her heart sank to her feet. Gran must be sick, life-threatening sick. And if Gran believed her time was up, she'd follow the creature without a fight.

Well, there was no way she was going to alert her to the grim's presence. She'd keep it a secret. She wasn't about to let Gran leave her, at least not anytime soon. She'd get her some healing help, and then everything would be okay. And with her haunt huntress talent and powers igniting any day now, maybe she'd even be the one to cure Gran.

But first, she had to get rid of the beast.

She hurried out of her room, casting another worried glance across the hall at the mumbling Gran busily packing her valise.

From the supply shelf, Evangeline grabbed the squirt bottle of chupacabra repellant. Grims and chupacabras cer-tainly weren't the same creature, but it was worth a try. She was hurrying back toward her room when she stopped. A white envelope lay on the kitchen counter, a white envelope bearing the broken wax seal of the council. She flipped it over. It was addressed to Gran, who would have told her to mind her own beeswax, but Evangeline didn't. She pulled out the letter and scanned its contents, furrowing her brow at the document's first line.

It is with unanimous agreement that the council approves your request to undertake the New Orleans case.

Gran had volunteered for the New Orleans job? And all eleven council members had agreed to this? But Gran disliked cities too. Unless . . . unless Gran knew her time was limited and she wanted to offer one last bit of assistance, as well as provide her apprentice one last training lesson.

Evangeline slipped the letter back into the envelope. Clutching the chupacabra repellent to her chest, she rushed to her room and closed the door after her.

Fader remained cowering under the bed. The black grim stood still an atone in the yard, staring toward the house. She slid the window up and streamed a healthy dose of the tangy-scented repellent at the beast, striking it on its black, tangled coat.

The big dog glanced around at its dampened fur, then, still not budging, turned its yellow gaze back toward the house.

Murmuring an appropriate chant, Evangeline thrust the sign of the evil eye at the creature. "I command you to leave these premises." She held her breath, hoping.

This time the beast turned away. With ears folded down and shoulders hunched, it silently plodded from the yard.

Exhaling a shaky sigh of relief, Evangeline closed the window. She knew her effort wouldn't hold, though. The grim would return. But maybe, just maybe, she'd managed to buy enough time for Gran to recover.

A crash of shattering glass sounded from across the hall. "Gran?" She spun away from the window and rushed to Gran's room.

A jar of Acadian fang worm venom lay scattered in shiny shards across the floor, the acidic poison chewing holes through the cypress-wood planks. Tiny tendrils of smoke curled up from the yellow stains. Gran was already kneeling, wiping up the spills with a thick towel beneath her work glove–protected hands and chastising herself for her slippery fingered clumsiness.

Evangeline went to help her clean, but Gran waved her away, motioning toward a row of miscellaneous-sized jars lined against the wall. "Run out and fetch more venom."

"But . . ." Evangeline searched for an excuse, any reason that would keep her from having to go. There were few chores she hated more than milking a full-grown Acadian fang worm. "You sure you don't want me to help you clean this?"

But Gran had finished wiping the mess away and was

climbing to her feet. "And don't dawdle," she admonished. She limped out with the smoking, sizzling towel to burn it in the backyard fire barrel.

Furrowing her brow, Evangeline watched her go. It wasn't like Gran to nervously drop anything, let alone a jar of hard-to-come-by ingredients. Gran wasn't the nervous type.

With a prickly fear jabbing her heart, Evangeline seized a small olive jar and dropped it into her satchel, adding it to the supply of vials and tiny jars already there. By the time she'd donned her dirty red hoodie and pulled on her satchel, Gran had returned, resuming her muttering and the packing of her valise.

Evangeline dipped the boat paddle into the bayou's tea-colored water, pulling it up and dipping it down again. Her small wooden pirogue slid past floating leaves, parting a trail through duckweed lying thick as a carpet of green confetti.

Navigating her way through a crowd of cypress tree knees poking up from the murky water like tiny wooden tombstones, she steered toward the bank, then hopped out. As she dragged the pirogue onto the muddy land, she ducked beneath a cottonmouth snake looped around the branch of a tree dripping with Spanish moss.

The snake stretched its jaws wide, baring the insides

of its cottony-white mouth as well as a set of shiny curved fangs, but Evangeline wasn't fazed. She was far more fearful of encountering a plot of greedy grass than tangling with a cranky water moccasin. The last thing she needed was to veer onto a patch of the cursed greenery and become stricken with a hunger so fierce, she'd resort to gnawing on her own fingers. Keeping her nose focused for the scent of sweet Ponchatoula strawberries would help. That's what greedy grass smelled like to her. Others might perceive a scent of okra or rice, or even bread pudding. The aroma was truly in the nose of the beholder.

Evangeline made her way deeper into the swamp, taking in her surroundings, wrapping them around her like a comfortable old shawl. Despite its multitude of lurking and slithering inhabitants, this was home. The thought of leaving this place for New Orleans brought a frowny pucker to her lips.

Rounding a dense tangle of undergrowth, she came to a toppled oak, victim to a rush of hurricane wind years ago, now rotted and teeming with insects. She paused, fixing her eyes on the downed tree, and listened carefully. Sure enough, a faint, wet slithering sound met her ears.

She pulled on her thick leather work gloves, knelt, and pushed aside a thorny blackberry bush.

There, inside the shady shelter, lay a clew of newly

hatched Acadian fang worms. A shaft of golden sunlight speared through the swamp's overhead branches, illuminating the nest and causing the tangle of young to squeal and mewl, their pale pink bodies not yet accustomed to the warmth of light. She grimaced at the squirmy sight, and at the odor—definitely not strawberries, more like soured, clumpy milk.

"Where are you?" Evangeline murmured. She swept her eyes around the shadowy lair, searching for the parent worm that was both mama and daddy, both male and female. It wouldn't have wandered far from its brood. She poked a stick into the rich black soil crawling with termites that served as nutritious food for the young, probing for a telltale lump indicating the sleeping adult. An angry hiss sounded behind her. She dropped the stick and whirled around.

Less than five yards away, a full-grown Acadian fang worm scooted out from beneath the tangle of undergrowth. The sight of the beast made her insides go squicky; the bruised color of their hides gave them the appearance of giant slithering intestines.

The two-and-a-half-foot-long creature reared up on its sausage-shaped body. Fatter and rounder than a snake, and far dumber, it opened its tiny, fang-lined mouth, aimed for her eyes, and spat.

Evangeline dove aside, shielding her face with her arm. The worm's venom splatted against the downed tree, singeing holes through the crumbling bark; a few drops of the corrosive matter flew onto the sleeve of her red hoodie, eating a series of holes through the fabric and causing her to mutter a curse word.

Keeping a wary eye on the giant worm as it flopped onto its belly and inched closer, she reached into her satchel and withdrew the tall, thin jar, its opening now covered with a rubber film rather than its metal lid. Gripping the container in one gloved hand, she waved her other at the approaching creature, back and forth in front of its beady eyes, hoping to befuddle it. "Come on now," she crooned. "Just a little bit closer."

When it had gotten within two feet of her, the fang worm reared up again, its head swaying to the motion of Evangeline's waving fingers.

Quick as a toad's tongue, she shot out her dancing hand and grasped the creepy crawly by the neck. "Gotcha!" she whispered. Before it could even think about spitting again, she rammed the jar to its wide-open mouth and forced its fangs through the rubber covering.

The monster thrashed back and forth, but Evangeline had a tight hold; its fury did not intimidate her at all. Wrinkling her nose at the unpleasant odor, she gave its jaw glands a squeeze, and drops of bright yellow venom slowly plopped into the glass.

After a painstaking length of time had passed, with her arm muscles aching and the jar satisfyingly half full, Evangeline released her grip on the creature's jaws, confident she'd extracted every last drop of acid it had to offer.

"Now that's how you milk an Acadian fang worm!" She grinned and shot a wink at the creature.

It gave her a sullen hiss in return. Knowing it had been beaten, it plopped onto its belly and crept beneath the log, back to the safety of its lair, back to protecting its young and building up another store of eye-blinding venom.

6

When Evangeline reached home an hour or so later, she handed the Acadian fang worm venom to Gran, who was seated at the front room table.

"Thank you, Evangeline." Gran took the jar, set it down beside her, and returned to the job of mixing, boiling, and bottling any fresh potions she might need for the New Orleans case.

Evangeline pulled out a chair across from her and plopped down onto it.

The tabletop lay cluttered with dried herbs and old tea tins. To Gran's left sat her mortar and pestle and an assortment of tongs, tweezers, and dented measuring spoons. To her right, a wooden box of cork-stoppered bottles, some filled with crystalized powders, others swirling with dark liquids. She measured out a spoonful of pulverized hookfoot claw and poured it into the brew simmering over an adjustable gas burner before her. After the resulting puff of smoke had cleared, she peered into the tiny cast-iron cauldron, then pursed her lips and furrowed her brow. "Evangeline, fetch my black book."

Evangeline climbed to her feet and went to the tall shelf packed tight with books of all widths and heights. Most of them had been passed down through the generations, their covers faded and fraying. To the casual observer the collection might have appeared disorganized, but Gran and Evangeline knew where each and every volume belonged. She tugged on the black one containing all Gran's original potion recipes, the one that would someday be donated to the Louisiana haunt huntress library when Gran's days were done.

The stained and spotted black book was wedged tight between *The Apprentice's Guide to Scrying* and the thick red volume of *Haunt Huntress History*. She gripped the spine with both hands and yanked, wrestling it free and sending the heavy leather volume of *HHH* shooting out after it. It thumped to the floor, splayed open and facedown.

Setting Gran's recipe book aside, she knelt beside the copy of *HHH*. She'd read through many of its pages over the years. It was the story of her family and of her ancestors.

Her own mama's name was listed in it a number of times in reference to the difficult cases she'd resolved, cases like the Nalusa Falaya. And the Terrebonne Troll. A beam of pride glowed inside her at the thought of being known as Josette Holyfield Clement's daughter and heir.

She lifted the book and flipped it over. The face of Celestine Bellefontaine stared back from one of the opened pages. Celestine Bellefontaine, the first and most powerful haunt huntress ever. The page on the opposite side recounted the story of her sixteen daughters, the branches from which all sixty-four Louisiana haunt huntress families had sprung, one for each of Louisiana's sixty four parishes.

Evangeline leafed through more pages, just as she did every time she opened the book, always searching for some fascinating nugget she hadn't noticed before. She paused at the section regarding the sage, the leader of all haunt huntresses. And even though she'd never met the current sage, it was one of her most returned-to sections. Not only was the sage the keeper of the haunt huntress library, which housed an assortment of dangerous magical artifacts, along with numerous books of wisdom written by haunt huntresses over the years, she also served as adviser and counselor. She was renowned for her wisdom, cleverness, and perceptive abilities. She was the most respected and revered of them all.

Her mama would have made a great sage.

"Evangeline?" Gran called. "My book?"

"Yes, ma'am." She closed the *Haunt Huntress History*, returned it to its place on the shelf, and delivered the potions book to Gran.

"Thank you, Evangeline. Now, go finish up the chores."

If there was one thing Gran just couldn't stand, it was going away on a trip and leaving the household chores undone.

With a sigh of dejection, Evangeline plodded toward the back door.

If there was one thing she just couldn't stand, it was having to do the household chores.

Grumbling to herself, Evangeline watered the herbs. She pulled weeds from the garden and sprayed it with cayenne pepper deer repellant. She made sure Guinevere the goat and the brood of nameless chickens were fed. Then she gathered the eggs from the coop. Inside the house she swept the floors and tidied the front room. She had just finished stirring the lootslang antivenin aging in a covered brass cauldron next to the hearth when her half brother, Percy, let himself in through the front door.

Percy, who was ten years older than Evangeline, shared the same daddy with her, but they'd been born to different mamas. And although he wasn't a direct descendant of Gran's, there was never any question he was her grandson and she was his grandmama. Family was family regardless of any differences in blood lines.

"Gran. Evangeline. How y'all doing?" Percy removed his camouflage ball cap, as he always did when entering the house. He crossed the room to Evangeline, where he gave her a hug, and she gave him one in return. Then he strode toward Gran, seated at the table. He kissed the top of her head as she pulled him in close.

"Look here." From behind his back Percy pulled out and proudly displayed a long-handled fishing net. "I modified this catfish net for y'all. For the next time you need to relocate a mess of them albino channel nixies. It's like a regular catfish net, see?" He swooped it through the air. "Only I replaced the string netting with aluminum wire. This way those dang nixies can't chew their way through and bite your fingers. You just dip it into an infested pond, scoop them out, and relocate them back to their home in the marsh."

Percy was always devising gadgets to assist Gran and Evangeline in their haunt hunts. Sometimes the gadgets worked. Sometimes they didn't.

"Thank you, Percy." Gran, who was still seated at the table, took the net and handed it to Evangeline, who put it in the chifforobe cabinet along with some of the other items he'd brought them.

"Hey there, Fader boy." Fader was rubbing circles around Percy's camouflage shrimp boots. Percy squatted and scratched him beneath the chin. Then he pulled a bit of gator jerky from the top pocket of his sleeveless flannel shirt and offered it to the grateful cat.

Gran wedged a cork stopper into a tube filled with an indigo-blue liquid. "We'll be ready to leave in just a few minutes."

As they rolled out of the swamp in Percy's rusted red pickup truck, Evangeline glanced out the back window, greatly wishing she could have stayed behind.

But she and Gran had a job to do. And haunt huntresses always helped when they were needed. She settled back, twisting her fingers together atop her lap.

Had her daddy been in town, maybe he would have been the one to drive them to New Orleans. But he was out in the Gulf on the oil rig where he always seemed to be working. She never held a grudge against him for his frequent absences, though. That was just the nature of his job: two weeks on and two weeks off.

Still, it would've been nice if they could've spent more time together. But even if he'd had a different job, she'd have been raised by Gran anyway. The mentor always raised the apprentice, training her in the skills of hunting haunts, homeschooling her in all the standard academic subjects, and teaching her the cures to any local supernatural afflictions.

There were also the endless incantations and protective patterns the mentor required her apprentice to memorize, as well as the instructing of more practical things, like how to navigate the bayou, how to climb trees, and how to fight.

Percy's slow-moving truck creaked and groaned as they rolled along. Percy kept up a steady chatter, always ending his stories with "Now, what do you think of that?" But she and Gran never got the opportunity to reply before he slid the toothpick from one side of his mouth to the other and launched into a new tale.

Evangeline shifted uncomfortably in the Sunday dress Gran had made her wear. Gran insisted they create a favorable first impression, but the dress was far from favorable to Evangeline. It made her itchy. At least she'd gotten to wear her boots and keep her bowie knife strapped to her leg, where it lay hidden beneath her skirt. And at least by going to New Orleans, they'd be putting some distance between themselves and the hateful grim, giving Gran a chance to recover from whatever was ailing her.

Evangeline listened to Percy's yarn spinning for a while

longer, then tuned him out, pondering what her haunt huntress talisman would look like. It would be custom-made and in the form of a silver circle, as they all were, ringed with a border of oak leaves, the symbol of strength. Cypress branches, representing perseverance through challenges, would fill the background. And at its center would sit a depiction of her animal familiar. Some people believed the talismans were magical, but the truth was, they contained no special powers other than the ability of their silver to ward off evil. They served more as a symbol of authenticity and accomplishment, a seal of the council's approval.

She touched her mama's talisman through the fabric of her dress. Its center bore the image of a hare. Her mama's familiar had been a jet-black hare with pearly-white eyes. A noble animal, no doubt, but if she could have her pick, hers would be a hawk, fierce and intelligent.

She peered out the truck's window, up at the blue-gray sky. Her familiar would show up any day now, presenting itself in the manner all haunt huntress familiars did: by resting its head against its mistress's feet. After it had done so, it would seldom leave her side, always there to protect and assist her.

As soon as she got back to the swamp, she would climb some oaks and nose around through the branches. Maybe her hawk familiar would be perched there, just waiting to present itself. She would stretch out her legs along one of the tree's sturdy limbs, and her familiar would hop down beside her to rest its majestic feathered head against the tips of her boots.

Evangeline smiled dreamily. And as soon as she secured her familiar, the only thing left was to prove to the council she "had heart," though she still wasn't sure how she was supposed to do that, or even what the term meant.

And with the acquisition of her familiar and her demonstration of heart, her haunt huntress powers would finally ignite inside her, her senses greatly enhanced, her intuition finely tuned. And in addition to those new abilities, she'd acquire her unique talent. It might be the capability to communicate with animals, or increased physical strength, or maybe even the power to heal through touch. Her own mama had been proficient in the art of scrying: She'd possessed a keen ability to divine hidden knowledge and future events by gazing into a reflective surface. Gran was a renowned potions and tonics master. Excitement fluttered inside Evangeline just thinking of all the possible talents her own might turn out to be.

Two hours and twenty-three minutes after they'd rolled out of the swamp, the brakes squealed, and the old pickup shuddered to a stop behind a shiny black convertible. The expensive-looking little car pulled away and sped off down the street, the male driver's short brown ponytail whipping out behind him.

"City folk," Evangeline grumbled, "with their fancy cars and their fancy sense of style."

Percy squinted up at the grand Garden District mansion, specifically at its address numbers. Squinting was another of his habits, since he was always losing his eyeglasses. "This is it." He put the truck into park, shut off the ignition, and stepped out, the door squealing as loudly as the brakes had.

As Gran and Evangeline climbed down, Percy hitched up his pants hanging loose on his lanky frame. He pushed the duck decoys, duck calls, and rubber boots out of the way, then pulled their suitcases from the truck bed. He hauled the luggage through a wrought-iron gate and up to the front porch.

The huge white house had so many columns and railings, and so much trim work, it looked like a wedding cake. It also sat on the corner. Evangeline frowned. Corner houses were unlucky. From the third-floor rooftop a crow cawed, and her heart lurched. A black bird perched on a housetop was a sure sign of death. She whispered a curse word.

"Language, Evangeline," Gran scolded.

With Fader tucked in her arm, Gran leaned into her cane and made her way up the front steps. Evangeline cast a worried glance at her, but Gran seemed perfectly fine.

Percy pushed the doorbell with the tip of his callused finger. Inside the huge house, the chimes sounded as majestically as church bells.

Still perched in Gran's arm, Fader reached a paw out to Percy and meowed.

"Okay, boy." Percy grinned and patted Fader's head. "One more for the road." He dipped his fingers into his shirt pocket, pinched off a piece of gator jerky, and offered it to the cat. Fader gobbled it up eagerly. Percy chuckled and scratched him between two of his four ears as Fader purred loudly. "That's good eatin' right there, ain't it, boy?"

Evangeline tugged at the starchy dress fabric. She reached around to give her backside a scratch, but a stern glance from Gran stayed her hand, and she smoothed out the skirt instead.

"Gran. Evangeline. Y'all have a nice stay." Percy gave each of them a peck on the cheek, gave Fader a final ear rub, then strolled down the steps. As he passed through the wrought-iron gate, he called over his shoulder, "Just let me know when I should come back and fetch you."

"Thank you, Percy," Gran said. "We'll send you a cardinal when it's time."

Evangeline waved him good-bye, watching wistfully as the old red truck bumped its way down the potholey street, growing smaller in the distance, until it was gone. She wished she were headed back to the swamp too. Even if it meant spending another two hours and twenty-three minutes with the yammering Percy and an itchy butt.

Fader yawned from his roost in Gran's arm. In a garden on the other side of the house, a fountain gurgled, and a blue jay whistled and chirped. Evangeline reached out to knock on the wide mahogany door, but Gran stopped her with her words. "Patience, Evangeline."

"Yes, ma'am." She let her hand drop to her side, doing her best to stand still and wait, two things she'd never been very good at. "Maybe they're not home. Maybe they left town," she offered hopefully.

The door latch clicked. Evangeline's hopes fell. The door eased open.

7

"**B**ack so soon, Laurent?" A man pulled the door the rest of the way open. "Did you forget something— Oh!" His smile faltered and his eyes widened. A flush of embarrassment tinged his face as well as his balding head. "Oh. I thought you were a friend of ours. . . . He just left. . . ." The man glanced from Gran to Evangeline, lingering for a second on her purple-bruised eye and the red scratch running down her cheek. His gaze shifted back to Gran, his mouth dropping open at the sight of the four-eared cat nestled in her arm. "Ah . . . Mrs. Holyfield. And you brought a . . . uh . . . pet with you."

"You allergic to cats, Mr. Midsomer?" Gran asked.

"Uh . . . no. No. Not at all." He stared at them for a moment longer, then stuck his head out the doorway and cast an uncomfortable glance up and down the street. With a smile that was just as uncomfortable, he quickly motioned for them to enter.

Evangeline was well aware of his kind—almost always residents of the big cities. They were scoffers when it came to believing in the abilities of people like her and Gran—that is, until they found themselves in desperate need of the services of people like her and Gran. Mr. Midsomer definitely looked like a scoffer in need.

Remembering his manners, Mr. Midsomer reached down. "Let me get your bags for you."

"That won't be necessary," Gran replied. "My apprentice will get them."

Evangeline frowned, not relishing the idea of lugging around Gran's heavy suitcase and valise as well as her own suitcase and satchel.

With Fader resting like royalty in the crook of her arm, Gran stepped into the foyer of the elegant house. The cat peered around at Evangeline, smirking as she struggled to haul the luggage inside. She narrowed her eyes and stuck out her tongue at him.

"Dignity, Evangeline," Gran chastised without turning her head. "A haunt huntress always maintains her dignity. No matter the situation."

"Yes, ma'am," Evangeline mumbled, and she followed

Gran into the huge, quiet foyer.

Mr. Midsomer quickly closed the front door and turned to face them. "It's uh, a pleasure to meet you, Mrs. Holyfield. Thank you for coming."

"It's my pleasure to meet you, Mr. Midsomer." Gran leaned her cane against the wall and held out her hand, and the man shook it. She motioned to Evangeline. "This is my granddaughter, Evangeline."

He gave a loud swallow. "Nice to meet you, Evangeline."

"Evangeline, my bag, please," Gran directed.

Evangeline passed her the heavy leather valise, and Gran handed her Fader.

As Gran rummaged around inside the bag, Evangeline dropped Fader to the shiny hardwood floor. He gave her a mild hiss of dissatisfaction and stalked away, stopping to sniff at the handwoven foyer rug.

"I didn't realize you'd be arriving so soon." Mr. Midsomer offered a weak smile. "I uh, wasn't expecting you until later tonight."

Gran paused in her search through her bag. "Didn't you receive my cardinal?"

"Ah . . . well, yes. We did have a bird that, uh . . ."

"Well, then," Gran said, "the note should have informed you of our change in plans and that we'd be arriving this evening between six and seven." She glanced at the antique grandfather clock ticking stoically against the wall. "It's now 6:29."

"Perhaps it would have been more convenient for you to have made a phone call." Mr. Midsomer offered another weak smile.

Gran waved her hand, dismissing the idea, and returned to rifling through her valise. "I try to avoid use of telephones, televisions, computers, and most electronics. They tend to drain one's mystic abilities, in addition to being unhealthily addictive. I also avoid motorized vehicles when possible, except for small outboard motors. Ah! Here it is." She pulled a bottle from her bag. Inside it swirled a dark, fudgy substance. But anyone who knew Gran knew it wasn't anything you'd want to pour over your ice cream.

She handed the bottle to Mr. Midsomer.

He hesitated a moment, then warily accepted it. "What is it?"

"A cure for baldness."

Mr. Midsomer's eyes widened. "Oh . . . ah . . . well . . ."

"It's just a mixture of garlic and pureed goose dung. Nothing to be afraid of. Sprinkle a few drops onto that bald patch twice a day. Make sure to rub it in good. Your hair will start sprouting within a week."

"Oh, no, thank you." He thrust the bottle back toward her.

"Would you rather a concoction of mouse droppings and honey? It takes a little longer, but works just as well, though it's a bit stickier." She peered into her bag. "I know I have a vial of it in here somewhere."

Mr. Midsomer gulped. "No. No. This will be fine. Thank you."

"My apologies, Mr. Midsomer!" A middle-aged woman rushed up the hallway, her face careworn and lined, the roots of her brown hair graying. She straightened the apron on her black uniform dress as she hurried past the fancy gold-framed paintings and antique side tables topped with oriental vases. "I was tending to the missus and didn't hear the doorbell."

"No need to apologize, Camille." Mr. Midsomer cleared his throat and held his hand out to introduce Gran. "This is Mrs. Midsomer's uh . . . new nurse, Mrs. Clotilde Holyfield."

Nurse? Evangeline opened her mouth, about to correct

him, when a sharp look from Gran snapped her lips shut.

"And her assistant, Evangeline." Mr. Midsomer turned to Gran as he motioned toward the frazzled woman in the black uniform dress. "This is our housekeeper, Camille Lyall. Now that you're here, Camille can return to her regular domestic duties. I'm afraid we've overworked her terribly these past few weeks with caring for my wife."

The housekeeper shook her head. "It's been no hardship, Mr. Midsomer." Her gaze fell upon Gran's silver haunt huntress talisman, and her eyes widened, but only for a fraction of a second. She quickly offered Gran a smile as warm as a fresh-baked biscuit. "How do you do, Mrs. Holyfield?"

"Camille, please show Mrs. Holyfield and her, uh . . . assistant to the guest room."

"Yes, Mr. Midsomer." Camille turned to Gran and Evangeline. "If you ladies will follow me." She tucked her hands into the front pockets of her apron and led them up the hallway to the grand wooden staircase.

Gran followed, clasping the banister in one hand and leaning into her cane with her other. Evangeline trailed after them, hauling along the suitcases and bags.

With a sympathetic shake of her head, Camille glanced back at Gran. "Arthritis, dear?" She sighed. "I tell you, some days getting up and down these stairs just takes all the fight out of me."

Arthritis? Evangeline scowled, disappointed when Gran didn't correct the woman's assumption. Gran had earned that injury in the line of haunt huntress duty. It had been a malicious . . .

Evangeline frowned deeper. Now that she thought about it, she didn't really know what species of creature it was that had nearly torn Gran's leg clean away all those years ago. A jolt of shame kicked her conscience. She'd simply never thought to ask Gran about it. It'd always just been a part of her, as much as the color of her eyes or the sound of her voice. Evangeline made a mental note to herself. She would ask Gran about it later. When the time was right.

Camille led them to a pleasantly pale-blue room furnished with a set of antique twin beds. A Persian rug covered the dark hardwood floor. "I hope you'll be comfortable here."

Gran replied she was sure they would be.

Evangeline was sure they would be too. "It's beautiful. The whole house is beautiful." She set down the bags and suitcases.

Camille nodded. "Mr. and Mrs. Midsomer made a lot of renovations to this old place when they moved here two years ago. Mrs. Midsomer decorated the entire house herself. She's very knowledgeable about antique furnishings. That's what brought them to New Orleans. She was hired on as manager of the Ardeas Antiques Gallery over on Royal Street." She waved a hand at them. "Oh, listen to me babbling on. I'll leave you to get settled in. Let me know if you need anything."

"Thank you, Miss Camille," Evangeline said. "We will."

Camille turned to leave, then paused. "I do have to say, I was a bit surprised Mr. Midsomer never mentioned your coming. Honestly, I never minded tending to the missus. I've been with the family only six months, but I've grown very fond of them." She offered an encouraging smile as she stepped from the room. "Rest up. You have a long night ahead of you." She pulled the door shut. Her footfalls faded away, down the lengthy hallway and then down the staircase.

Gran drew aside the gauzy white curtains and peered through the window's wavy old glass. She cast a troubled glance at the lowering sun.

It wasn't often that Gran looked worried. One of the earliest lessons every haunt huntress learned was how to keep her fear concealed. Evangeline squeezed her fingers against her suddenly sweaty palms. "Gran? What's wrong?"

Gran turned away from the window and lay down on one of the beds, right on top of the covers. She folded her hands over her chest, shutting one eye and focusing the other on Evangeline. "I suggest you take a rest. Things are going to get rough tonight, and we'll need our energy."

But Evangeline didn't feel the least bit sleepy. What she felt was a little annoyed and a lot curious. Back home, Gran had been too busy to reveal the job details. And of course, they couldn't speak about the subject on the truck ride over. Haunt huntresses never discussed the particulars of a case in front of others, not even family members. "Gran? What's our job here?"

"We'll talk about it after I've had my nap."

Evangeline opened her mouth, about to protest, then snapped her lips shut. Gran would tell her when she was good and ready to tell her, and not a moment before.

Taking a seat on the other bed, Evangeline removed her bowie knife and sheath and set them on the nightstand. With a sigh, she lay down. She closed her eyes, and her dark doubts came speeding into her head, rattling through her brain like the fully loaded cars of a freight train: What if she turned thirteen and her familiar still had not shown up? What if not even the tiniest hint of haunt huntress power ever emerged? What if she really was a middling? What if Gran couldn't be cured? She threw her eyes open and sat up, shaking her head. No. She wouldn't think about those things right now. She climbed out of bed, fastened her knife and sheath back onto her leg, and eased the door open.

Leaving Gran snoring softly, she stepped into the hallway and clicked the door shut behind her.

She'd just do a little looking around. After all, a good haunt huntress took initiative and always assessed her surroundings. Maybe she'd try to get a peek at Mrs. Midsomer, see for herself what was ailing her.

Evangeline wandered down the hallway, scratching her itchy backside and observing the expensive-looking side tables, vases, and framed artwork, feeling like a fish out of water among such fine furnishings inside such a big ritzy house. As she strolled, she pondered the possibilities of what Mrs. Midsomer's condition might be. Perhaps she'd had a Moonstroke. Or she could be suffering from Couchemar Syndrome—experiencing persistent sleep paralysis was a terribly unpleasant condition. Maybe it was a severe case of Grunch Rash. Possibly Fifolet Burn, or even Chasse-Galerie Tinnitus.

Halfway down the hall, she came to a narrow set of stairs. A closed door waited at the top. She probably shouldn't go up. She put a foot on the first tread, and it creaked. She paused, her heart slightly pounding. No one came running to tell her she shouldn't be there. She put a foot on the second creaky step, and, casting a last glance over her shoulder, she made her way up and opened the door.

She'd just take a quick look around and then leave.

Some people might say she was being nosy. She preferred to think she was being sensible.

A flip of the wall switch lit a lamp next to a towering bookcase lined with books and small wooden models of catapults and other assorted medieval weaponry. In the center of the windowless room stood a round table scattered with screwdrivers, magnifying glasses, paintbrushes, and a homemade wooden crossbow. The room's simple furnishings eased her out-of-place discomfort, but only a little.

On a nearby wall, nestled among a series of superhero posters, hung a framed family photo. She recognized Mr. Midsomer right away, though based on his full head of black hair, the picture must have been taken years ago. Beside him sat a dark-haired, olive-complexioned woman with eyes as blue and piercing as those of a leucistic alligator. On her lap, she held a pale and fair-haired little boy who looked to be about three or four years old.

The woman was beautiful, and Evangeline's eyes kept going back to her. A pang echoed through her heart. Her mama had been pretty too, maybe not quite as elegant as this woman, but that didn't matter. Her mama had been an accomplished haunt huntress. There weren't many who could be credited with singlehandedly clearing out an infestation of graveyard ghouls like her mama had done.

She pulled her fingers away from her mama's silver

talisman at her neck, not realizing she'd put her hand there in the first place.

A haunt huntress needed to stay focused when on a job, even if she didn't know exactly what that job was. She took a magnifying glass from the cluttered table and brought it up to the family photo. Maybe there was something here she could learn about Mrs. Midsomer.

"Who are you?" a voice asked from a shadowy corner across the room.

Evangeline whirled around, dropping the magnifying glass as her hand went to her knife.

A boy about her age moved out of the shadows near the tall bookcase. He stared at her from behind what she considered to be a slightly large nose.

"Where'd you come from?" she blurted. How had she not seen him there a moment before? A haunt huntress always assessed her surroundings for living and nonliving beings before entering a room.

The boy stepped into the lamplight. "This is my workroom."

He looked unhealthily pale, but then again, most city folk did. Judging by his neatly cut blond hair and his expensive-looking loafers, Evangeline assumed he must be Mr. and Mrs. Midsomer's son.

"Who are you?" he demanded again.

Her embarrassment at being discovered sent her thoughts and words stuttering. "I . . . I'm Evangeline Clement."

"I don't like people touching my belongings. Return my magnifying glass to its proper place."

"Huh?" She cast a puzzled glance at the messy table, having no idea where it belonged.

"Between the yellow-handled screwdriver and the tube of superglue."

She scooped the magnifier from the floor and scurried to the table, about to comply, when she paused. No. She would not replace it where she'd found it. This boy was rude, and she did not cooperate with rudeness. Not if she didn't have to. She set it between a paintbrush and a box of Q-tips instead.

"Why do you smell like the herb rosemary?"

Another flare of embarrassment ignited inside Evangeline, but she quickly extinguished it. She straightened her shoulders and lifted her chin. "The aroma of rosemary brings its wearer good luck."

"You don't have many friends, do you?"

Evangeline furrowed her brow. "Because I smell like rosemary?"

"Because your hand went for what I infer is a knife strapped to your left leg, an action that would cause most

potential friends a great deal of anxiety." He gave a casual shrug. "I don't have many friends either. I'm rather particular about who I choose to spend my time with."

Before she could reply, not that she had a reply ready, the boy fired off more questions. "What do you want? Why are you in my room? Are you one of Camille's relatives?"

"No." Evangeline shook her head. "I'm here with my gran to take care of the lady of the house. My gran's a . . . a nurse. And I'm here to help out with . . . thermometers and ice packs and stuff." She smiled, but she knew it was strained. Gran always said her natural smile could dazzle starlight itself, but not to bother with her fake one because it looked as gruesome as a ghoul's.

"Father didn't tell me the shaman woman would bring a little girl with her."

Evangeline's mouth fell open, but only for a fraction of a second. Then she drew herself up. "Well, Gran didn't tell me the Midsomers had a little boy."

Her comment didn't have the withering effect she'd intended. The boy's expression remained impassive as he studied her face. "You don't look like a smoke detective."

"I . . . a what?"

"A smoke detective. It's a term I coined. It means one who chases things that don't exist. A person who communes with spirits. A man or woman who practices faith healing.

A mystic, a spiritualist, a medium, a witch doctor, a sage, a healer. Father is at his wits' end and has apparently resorted to hiring such charlatans." The boy's tone wasn't accusatory. Had it been, Evangeline might have taken a swing at him.

"Gran and I are *not* charlatans. We are haunt huntresses. Some people might call us swamp witches, but we are *not* charlatans." She stabbed a finger at him. "We're the women people like you call for help when ghosts, monsters, and other assorted haunts get up to no good." She took a step forward, keeping her finger directed at him. "We're the ones who send those creatures back where they belong, whether that be the mist-shrouded graveyard, the murky depths of the bayou, or even the fiery-frozen pits of hell itself." She gave an indignant huff, then shot him a glare for good measure.

"Which means you're not really nurses."

Dang it! She'd said too much. She did not like this boy. Not at all.

"What happened to your face?"

The tips of Evangeline's ears burned scarlet. "What do you mean?"

"You have a contusion near your eye and a laceration along your cheek."

"I . . . It's none of your business what happened to my face."

Gran would have given her a disapproving look for such a rude comment. A tiny wave of shame lapped at the edge of her conscience. But if the boy had been insulted, he didn't show it.

"I'm glad your laceration has scabbed over. I don't care much for the sight of blood." He walked to the table and moved the magnifying glass to its correct place.

Finally, Evangeline had the upper hand. "You're afraid of blood?" She didn't even try to suppress her smirk.

"The sight of blood makes me extremely uncomfortable, as do ventriloquists' dummies, hair clumps in sink drains, the possibility of a sudden reversal in the earth's gravitational force, and the possibility of contracting a brain tumor from radiofrequency waves. I also have a fear of waking from an anesthesia-induced coma, only to discover my face has been permanently painted with mime's makeup."

Evangeline mentally sifted through the contents of Gran's valise, though she doubted even the most potent of Gran's tonics could cure what was wrong with this boy.

A high-pitched beeping broke the silence. He pressed a button on his watch. "Ah, dinnertime."

"You need to be reminded when to eat?"

"I set my watch alarm for all the important events of my evening. Seven p.m. is dinner. Eight p.m. is model painting. Nine p.m. is when I watch *Dr. Who*. Eleven p.m. is reading time, and midnight is lights-out. I find an orderly life to be a more productive life, don't you?"

"What about ten p.m.?" Evangeline cocked an eyebrow, certain she had caught a mistake in the know-it-all boy's schedule.

He gave her a disdainful look, as though the answer were perfectly obvious. "If I watch *Dr. Who* at nine p.m., it will end at ten p.m., which will clearly indicate it is then time to brush my teeth, shower, and put on my pajamas."

Evangeline shook her head, at a loss for how to reply to something so nonsensical.

He focused his gaze on her feet. "Why are the tips of your boots silver? Does it have something to do with one of the quaint superstitions of your people?"

Oh, but this city boy was pushing her too far. She glanced at the family photo on the wall and back to the boy. "You don't look anything like your parents."

"The reason I don't look like them is that I was adopted; therefore, I share none of their genetics. My father is of Italian and Romanian descent. My mother's ancestry can be traced to South Asia, as well as Spain, France, and Morocco. Based upon my fair skin and eyes, I'm most likely of Scandinavian descent. Your comment regarding our dissimilar appearances, though accurate, was a rude one."

Evangeline's face steamed with shame. All she wanted

to do at that moment was climb beneath a floorboard and disappear. "I'm sorry. I didn't mean to make you feel bad." She had no idea what else she could say to soften her offense.

"You didn't make me feel bad." He shrugged. "It's simply a fact of genetics. Facts are truths, and it's illogical to feel bad about truths. I was just relaying a helpful social cue so you can avoid insulting others in the future."

Her emotions were flipping and flapping like a stop sign in a hurricane. She didn't know how to reply. Not for the first time in her life, she wished she had a familiar at her side. Then maybe it would attack him, and she wouldn't have to feel guilty about it.

The boy continued. "I possess a keen sense of bluntness. I've had to teach myself what's considered rude and what's not so I won't inadvertently offend others. My expressed truths are often mistaken as insults."

Evangeline stepped toward the door. "I have to go."

"There's a bathroom at the foot of the stairs. It's the first door on the right."

"No! I didn't mean I needed to go to . . ." Evangeline shook her head. "I meant I have to leave. I have—"

Footsteps mounted the stairs outside the room, the treads creaking. A delicious smell wafted ahead of the climber, and Evangeline's stomach growled loudly and embarrassingly.

Camille entered carrying a tray containing a plate of

chicken nuggets, a white ramekin cup of ketchup, a second ramekin containing three carrot sticks, a can of Coke, a fork, and a white cloth napkin. "Oh, hello, Miss Evangeline. I see you've met Julian." She set the tray on a TV table next to a large chair.

The boy, Julian, took a seat, and his eyes grew wide. "Are you injured?" He pointed at Camille's left hand. "You're not bleeding, are you?" He leaned away from her, glaring suspiciously at the Band-Aid attached to her inner wrist.

Camille waved away his concern. "I nicked myself with a kitchen knife—nothing to get all worked up about. It's little more than a scratch really."

Julian cast a horrified glance at the ramekin of carrot sticks, his face going pale.

"Oh, for goodness' sakes. It happened *after* I prepared your meal, while I was washing up the dishes."

Julian's shoulders relaxed, but he still peered closer at the carrots.

Camille shook her head and rolled her eyes, then gave Evangeline a smile. "Your grandmother requests your presence in your room."

"Yes, ma'am." Evangeline nodded, grateful for the excuse to get away.

Seeming satisfied that the carrot sticks were up to his sanitary standards, Julian snatched up the fork and stabbed a chicken nugget.

"Now, don't go wolfin' down your food," Camille admonished. "You know how that upsets your stomach and gives you gas."

Evangeline rushed down the staircase. Remembering her manners as Gran had taught her, she called out behind her, "It was nice meeting you, Julian."

Even though it wasn't.

She bounded down the last two steps, hurried into the long hallway, then slowed, not sure which of the many closed doors belonged to her and Gran's room. She tapped against the one nearest to her. "Hello?"

When no one answered from the other side, she eased the door open and peered into a disheveled scene. "Heavens to Betsy," she murmured. The bed was unmade, covers rumpled, and pillow on the floor. An empty chip bag and soda can sat on the nightstand. A maid's uniform hung over the back of a chair. It must be Camille's room. Scattered across the dresser lay a brush, a comb, an opened box of Band-Aids, and a very loud and very ugly paisley-print scarf.

Evangeline closed the door and moved on, pausing at the next one. She raised her hand to knock.

"Did you lose your way, Miss Evangeline?" Camille called from the end of the hallway.

Evangeline turned with an embarrassed grin. "Yes, ma'am. I sure did."

"Right this way, my dear." Camille led her along. "Mr. Midsomer's giving me the night off now that you and your gran are here, but I'll be back first thing tomorrow morning." She cleared her throat, hesitating. "Miss Evangeline, I feel I must confess something."

"Yes, ma'am?" Evangeline wasn't sure she wanted to hear what Camille had to say. Confessions usually involved the revelation of some sort of uncomfortable information.

"I know you and your gran aren't really nurses, at least not in the traditional sense." Camille glanced around to make sure they were alone. "Mr. Midsomer has a hard time believing in the supernatural, but I know there are things in this world that fall beyond logical explanation. I just wanted you to know you and your gran's secret is safe with me. I want nothing but health, renewed strength, and long life for my beautiful mistress."

Evangeline made up her mind right then and there that she liked Camille, certainly far better than she liked Julian Midsomer.

Camille stopped before a closed door and motioned toward it. "Here we are."

"Thank you. Gran and I will do our best to get Mrs. Midsomer back to herself again."

"And don't you worry none about what might happen with the missus tonight," Camille added. "I suppose her actions might seem frightening to those not used to such patients, but I probably don't need to caution you, considering your line of business." She gave Evangeline a parting wink and walked away.

Evangeline opened the bedroom door, and the musty odor of dried chrysanthemums filled her nose.

Gran sat at the room's antique writing desk, using her mortar and pestle to grind up the dried flower heads. Some of the contents of her valise lay splayed across the bed—bags of willow bark, bay leaves, and spider legs alongside bottles of bindweed, powdered antler tips, mistletoe, rye, and aconitum.

Before Evangeline pulled the door shut, Fader trotted in after her with a large flying cockroach clutched in his mouth. He jumped onto Gran's bed and dropped the dead bug beside the assortment of bottles.

"Thank you, Fader," Gran said.

Fader stuck his hind leg into the air and began grooming himself.

"Evangeline, take care of that for me, please."

"Yes, ma'am."

"And run a comb through your hair. We're going down to dinner as soon as I'm done here."

Evangeline peered into the dresser mirror. Her hair looked okay to her. Aside from her bruised eye and scratched cheek, she figured she looked presentable enough. She fetched an empty vial from Gran's bag, and using a pair of tweezers, she took the insect by one of its wilted wings and dropped it inside. It'd come in handy later if they needed to make a roach tea for someone afflicted with lockjaw.

Gathering her courage, she turned and faced Gran. She'd been patient long enough. If Gran gave her the brush-off again, this time she would insist that she trust her enough to give her the answer. "Gran? Are you going to tell me why we're here?"

"I'm sorry, Evangeline. I've just been preoccupied with preparing and planning." Gran dumped the contents of the mortar into a paper packet and folded it shut. With a sigh, she rose from the desk. She poured a mound of dry cat food into Fader's bowl, then began repacking the bags and bottles into her valise. "I'm not sure what's wrong with Mrs. Midsomer, only that she's been very ill the past three weeks, and that she grows weaker every day. The medical doctors can't seem to figure it out."

"Oh. Is that all?" Evangeline almost felt let down.

Gran arched an eyebrow at her.

"I mean, maybe she's possessed by a ghost. Or a demon."

"Could be." Gran snapped her valise shut. "But I don't want to start speculating until I get a look at her for myself." She opened the door and ushered Evangeline out.

They made their way down the stairs, Gran descending slowly ahead of her, holding on to the railing and using her cane to help her along. Fear pinched Evangeline's heart. When had Gran become so old and frail? *Hang in there, Gran. Soon the council will declare me an official haunt huntress, and I'll start taking care of you. Then you can retire and do nothing but take it easy.*

When they entered the dining room, Evangeline nearly gasped. She'd never eaten in a room so fancy. A sparkling crystal chandelier dripped from the ceiling. A gleaming silver tea service sat on a tray on top of the antique polished mahogany buffet. The tall windows wore velvet drapes so lengthy that their excess cloth flowed onto the floor.

She and Gran took their seats at the long table, on satin-covered chairs not at all practical for the dusty, muddy bottoms of working-class folk.

Mr. Midsomer entered and set a covered platter on the tabletop.

At the sight of it, Evangeline's stomach growled. She

was so hungry she could've eaten an entire pot of red beans along with a loaf of French bread and still had room left for a great big bowl of banana pudding.

"Camille's taking a much-deserved evening off, so I've cooked dinner for us," Mr. Midsomer announced proudly. "Filet mignon. Fresh from the patio grill."

Evangeline cast her eyes over the table set with linen place mats, china plates, and crystal goblets. Obviously, Camille had laid everything out beforehand. She couldn't imagine a man who'd cooked dinner outside would've gone to such formal extremes inside. Which also meant poor Camille would be greeted with a stack of dirty dishes when she returned tomorrow morning. Maybe she'd surprise the nice housekeeper and clean things up for her.

Mr. Midsomer removed the cover from the platter, revealing the grilled meat—small, round and brown, nearly three inches high, crisscrossed with black sear marks, and looking suspiciously pink beneath its glistening exterior. He inhaled the fleshy aroma. "Ahh."

Evangeline's stomach flopped like a fish on dry land. If there was one food she simply couldn't abide, it was under-cooked meat.

Using a set of tongs, he plunked a filet onto Gran's plate and then one onto Evangeline's. "I hope you like them bloody."

Evangeline stared down at the questionable hunk of

beef, wishing she were gazing down at a plate of golden fried catfish, hush puppies, and creamy green coleslaw instead. She glanced around the tabletop. "Isn't there anything else to go with it?"

"Evangeline!" Gran scolded.

Mr. Midsomer gazed at the undercooked steak. "I uh, I would have baked some potatoes, but my son, Julian, used all of them to test one of his new trebuchet models. He uh . . ." Mr. Midsomer paused and cleared his throat uncomfortably. "He uh . . . catapulted them over the backyard fence." He gave a dejected sigh, then added, "I would have prepared a salad too, but he also launched the tomatoes . . . as well as the head of lettuce."

Evangeline shook her head sadly. That boy had more problems than a math book.

"Julian's always thinking outside the box, a very beneficial asset to possess." Mr. Midsomer forced a tight smile, as though trying to reassure himself.

While Gran carved into her filet with her knife and fork, revealing an inside the color of strawberry cake, Mr. Midsomer held up a bottle of wine. "Merlot?"

"Yes, please," Gran replied.

He filled her crystal goblet with the blood-red beverage. "Evangeline, what can I get you to drink?"

"Just water." Evangeline frowned down at the undercooked hunk of meat.

Gran cleared her throat meaningfully.

"Just water, *please*," Evangeline corrected herself.

Mr. Midsomer excused himself from the table and a moment later returned with a green tear-shaped bottle. He filled the crystal goblet before her. The liquid fizzled and bubbled like clear Coca-Cola.

It was the strangest water Evangeline had ever seen. She took a sip and grimaced. It was also the strangest water she'd ever tasted. She let the sip dribble back into the glass and wiped her mouth on her dress sleeve.

Mr. Midsomer cleared his throat. "Evangeline, I hear you've met Julian."

"Yes, sir, I did." She paused, struggling to find something nice to say about the persnickety boy. "He, uh, certainly seems to like building those wooden models."

"Oh, yes," Mr. Midsomer agreed. "He has quite the interest in model making . . . this month." He forced another tight smile. "Julian's had many hobbies over the past year: soapmaking, yarn bombing, turnip carving, collecting those little stickers they put on bananas, making shoes out of duct tape . . ."

Evangeline couldn't fault the boy for having a penchant for duct tape. Percy was often using it to repair broken parts on his pickup truck.

Mr. Midsomer cut off a bite of steak and raised it to his mouth. "I apologize that Julian's not able to join us. He prefers to take his dinners in his workroom."

"No need to apologize, Mr. Midsomer," said Gran. "We're here on business, not to socialize."

As Gran and Mr. Midsomer went on to eat and make polite conversation, which seemed a lot like socializing to Evangeline, she stared down at her plate.

When Mr. Midsomer had finished his steak, he wiped the corners of his mouth with his white linen napkin. "Mrs. Holyfield, perhaps your granddaughter would like to retire to her room, so we might discuss my wife's . . . uh . . . treatment."

If Evangeline had been a cat, her fur would have bristled. She opened her mouth to protest, but Gran spoke before she could sputter her first word of objection.

"Evangeline's my assistant. She stays with me. I assure you, you can trust in her discretion."

Mr. Midsomer nodded. He took a deep breath and then took a sip of wine. He shifted in his chair. He tugged on his earlobe. "I feel you should know, I uh . . . I don't believe in religious or supernatural phenomena. It was a friend of mine, a professor of folklore studies at the University of Louisiana, who recommended I seek your help. I've had nearly every medical specialist in the state examine my wife, but no pill, therapy, or procedure has worked. I even asked for help from a friend who's an herbalist, but he couldn't cure her either. She grows weaker every day and suffers most terribly at night with . . . well, you'll soon see." He rubbed the sides of his face and sighed wearily. "I don't believe in your line of work." He looked up, right into Gran's eyes, and his voice cracked when he spoke. "But I don't know where else to turn."

"That's okay." Gran gave him a pat on his arm. "You don't have to believe for our methods to work."

Mr. Midsomer offered her a grateful smile. His hand shook as he refilled his glass, and a trickle of red wine dribbled onto the tabletop.

Evangeline winced. Spilling wine was a sign of bad luck.

An unearthly shriek sounded from down the hall, freezing Evangeline's blood and raising the tiny hairs on the back of her neck.

Mr. Midsomer glanced out the window at the setting sun. He looked wearier and more broken than any man Evangeline had ever seen, as though his heart had been snapped right in two.

The terrified shriek sounded again, so out of place in the beautiful, stately mansion.

"Well, let's get to it." Gran pulled her napkin off her lap and set it on the table. Tucking her talisman inside the neck of her dress, she rose and grabbed her cane.

Evangeline's insides writhed like a tangle of earthworms. Her stomach grew queasy despite her not having eaten anything.

With a sad sigh, Mr. Midsomer showed Gran from the dining room. Evangeline followed, grabbing the wine cork from the tabletop and dropping it into her dress pocket. She'd add it to Gran's supplies later. A cork wasn't just useful as a token of good luck. When placed underneath a pillow, it was also quite helpful in warding off intestinal cramps.

The three of them made their way down the wide hallway and toward the back of the house, Gran's cane tapping along the hardwood floor like a clock ticking toward the thirteenth hour.

Mrs. Midsomer's bedroom was fit for a queen. Lush rug, antique paintings, velvet drapes. The mahogany four-poster bed she rested on was so large, the entire Arseneau family could have slept in it with room to spare for their four hunting dogs. Mrs. Midsomer lay tucked beneath the white silk covers, her eyes closed. And despite her slightly sunken cheeks, Evangeline thought she still looked very beautiful.

Camille sat at the bedside, brushing the woman's long black hair.

"Camille?" Mr. Midsomer raised his eyebrows in surprise. "I thought you'd gone."

"I was just finishing up a few things, Mr. Midsomer." She set the hairbrush aside. "I wanted to make sure everything was in order for the new nurses."

"Thank you," Gran said. "My assistant and I can take over from here."

"I don't mind staying a bit longer if you'd like." Camille patted Mrs. Midsomer's perspiring forehead with a white cotton cloth. "Just until you get better acquainted with the missus."

"That won't be necessary," Gran said. "You go on. We'll take good care of her."

Camille set the cloth aside and rose from the bedside chair. "Are you sure?"

"We're sure." Gran gave her a terse nod.

"If you need me—"

"We won't." Gran held her hand out toward the door.

"Well. Good night, then." Camille gave them a parting nod, and casting a last look back at her patient, she left the room.

"Amala." Mr. Midsomer drew his wife's slender hand from beneath the blanket. Threading his fingers between hers, he leaned close. "Amala, this is Clotilde Holyfield, and her granddaughter Evangeline. They've come to help you."

When she didn't respond, he repeated her name.

Her eyes fluttered open, and he stumbled back, dropping her hand.

Mrs. Midsomer gazed at him for a moment before

recognition filled her bright-blue eyes. "Did you say something, John? Or was I dreaming?"

He took her hand again, relief settling over his face. "I've brought Mrs. Holyfield and her granddaughter, Evangeline, to see you. They're here to help you get better."

"Mrs. Holyfield. Elizabeth." She spoke the names as though trying to commit them to memory.

"It's Evangeline, ma'am," Evangeline corrected her. "My name's Evangeline."

"Evangeline. You're very kind. Thank you for coming." Mrs. Midsomer glanced past them, sweeping her gaze around the room as though searching for someone else.

Mr. Midsomer cleared his throat. "Julian sends his love."

Oh, I seriously doubt that. Evangeline fought back a frown of skepticism. If that boy had any love for his mama, he should be here bringing it himself.

Mrs. Midsomer's face brightened, and she squeezed Mr. Midsomer's hand. "How is Julian today?" Her slight smile revealed a heart brimming with affection. "Has he finished that new crossbow?"

"If you want, ma'am, I can go fetch him and bring him here to see you." Evangeline motioned toward the bedroom doorway.

"No." The light in Mrs. Midsomer's face dimmed ever so slightly. "It's best for him not to visit during the evenings.

It hurts him to see me this way. Especially when . . ." The corners of her mouth turned down. "Especially when I have an outburst. He does come to see me, though." Her face lit again. "Every day after school he sits and reads aloud while I sleep." She gazed toward the copy of *Pride and Prejudice* sitting on the nightstand.

A bookmark protruding from between its covers indicated only a few pages remained before they reached the story's end. Evangeline didn't know for sure, but it certainly appeared to be a sad omen.

"Julian can't stand *Pride and Prejudice*." Mrs. Midsomer smiled wistfully.

"Then why does he read it?" Evangeline asked.

"Because I adore *Pride and Prejudice*."

Evangeline's eyebrows shot up before she could stop them. Maybe, just maybe, Julian wasn't *quite* as pigheaded as she'd supposed.

"And even though I'm asleep"—Mrs. Midsomer's words slowed, and her voice grew fainter—"I hear every word he reads about Elizabeth and Mr. Darcy." Her eyes grew droopy, and Evangeline barely heard her when she murmured, "He's really not as disagreeable as many people believe him to be. He has a good and caring heart, even if he doesn't always show it in the normal ways."

Evangeline wasn't sure if she was referring to the fictional

Mr. Darcy or Julian. She thought on it for a moment, then decided Mrs. Midsomer most surely had meant the man in the book.

Mrs. Midsomer's eyes closed, and her breathing grew relaxed and steady, but Evangeline doubted things would stay this way for long.

Mr. Midsomer remained by the side of the bed, clutching his wife's hand and resting his sad gaze on her. He ran his other hand through his thinning hair. "I was away on business a month ago, only for a few days. And when I returned, she was already so ill. Feverish and shivering, always wrapped in a blanket or sweater."

Taking him by the arm, Gran tugged him away and escorted him to the bedroom door. "Let us do our work. We'll let you know if we need anything."

He paused, looking a bit like a lost child. "You'll take good care of her, won't you?"

"We will." Gran shooed him off, and with head and shoulders bowed, he moved away and left them to their work.

Mrs. Midsomer gasped. Her eyes flew open, and she stared up at Evangeline and Gran, her gaze round and terrified. Her mouth opened and closed as though she desperately wanted to tell them something but had forgotten how to speak.

The sight stirred a mixture of pity and horror within Evangeline.

"Evangeline, what do you see?" asked Gran, ever the teacher.

Evangeline snapped to. She had a job to do. She swept her gaze around, taking in the crystal vases of pleasantly scented white roses placed throughout the lavish room. On the fancy French-style dresser sat a copy of the same family photo she'd seen hanging on the wall of Julian's workroom. She turned her focus to Mrs. Midsomer. Despite her being bedridden for over three weeks, her hair was brushed to a shiny gleam. Unlike her appearance in the family photo, her complexion was now pale and drawn, and dark circles ringed her eyes, but her gown and bedding were as clean as fresh-fallen snow. Whatever was going on, one thing was certain: Mrs. Midsomer was very well cared for and very loved.

Beneath the covers, Mrs. Midsomer's arms and legs suddenly shot outward, her limbs as straight and stiff as if they'd been made of wood. She screamed another blood-curdling scream.

Evangeline wanted to squeeze her eyes shut and cover her ears, but that was not the haunt huntress way. Haunt huntresses were strong, capable of facing whatever unpleasant circumstances a job presented.

Panting short, rapid breaths, Mrs. Midsomer closed her

eyes. She moved her lips, murmuring words Evangeline did not understand. She glanced to Gran for an interpretation, but Gran's mouth was drawn tight, her eyes studying the woman.

Mrs. Midsomer spoke again, and this time her words were clear as glass. "I'm sorry." Her eyes opened and filled with a sorrowful lucidity. "I'm sorry."

Gran patted her hand. "It's okay, honey."

With a grateful smile, the woman closed her eyes again, and this time, she slept.

"Is it a case of Moonstroke, Gran?" Evangeline's heart thudded so hard, the vibrations knocked against her eardrums.

"No." Gran shook her head. "Evangeline, go fetch my bag, please."

"Yes, ma'am." Evangeline shot off, up the stairs and down the hall, and almost ran right into Camille as she stepped out of her room.

"Oh! Miss Evangeline, you startled me!" Camille pulled the door closed. She straightened her black uniform dress, patted her hair into place, then adjusted the unattractive paisley-print scarf tied at her throat. A silver choker-style necklace peeked out beneath it, thick and plain and ugly. Evangeline tried not to grimace. She herself certainly wasn't anything close to being stylish, but poor Camille had no taste at all in fashion.

"Excuse me." Evangeline motioned toward her and Gran's room. "Gran needs her bag."

Camille smiled. "I'll see you tomorrow, dear."

Evangeline dashed to their room. She slung her satchel over her shoulder, grabbed Gran's old valise, and dashed back out, passing Camille on her way down the staircase.

Evangeline handed Gran her bag. Mrs. Midsomer's eyes were still closed, but she tossed her head from side to side. Gran pulled a pungent garlic poultice from the valise and dabbed the woman's neck and forehead, to calm her hysterics in addition to giving her an extra boost of protection from evil.

"Rye, please." Gran held out her hand.

Evangeline dug through Gran's bag and passed a stalk to her.

Gran placed the piece of grass on the white pillow. Mrs. Midsomer whipped her head away from it. Gran removed the stalk and gave it to Evangeline. "Mistletoe."

Evangeline pulled out a dark-green sprig and passed it to Gran, who held it two feet above Mrs. Midsomer's head. Mrs. Midsomer moaned and raised her hands, trying to swipe it away. Gran handed the mistletoe to Evangeline. "Silver, please."

Evangeline hesitated. Showing a similar aversion to silver would not bode well for Mrs. Midsomer. Silver was one of the most powerful forces in nature. Its touch was capable of causing excruciating pain to those possessed by evil, the very reason haunt huntresses kept their silver talismans hidden inside their shirt or dress collars when dealing with such afflicted patients.

"Evangeline?" Gran glanced over at her. "The silver, please."

"Yes, ma'am." Evangeline rummaged around in the bag, took out the doubloon, and passed it to Gran.

Pinching the coin between her thumb and index finger, Gran lowered it toward Mrs. Midsomer's forehead. Long before it could make contact with flesh, the woman let out a shriek and slapped Gran's arm away.

A curse word slipped from Evangeline.

"Language, Evangeline." Gran furrowed her brow, muttering to herself, then returned the doubloon to Evangeline.

"Should I sprinkle holy water in the room's corners, to keep any more demons away?"

Gran kept her gaze on Mrs. Midsomer, who'd resumed her rapid panting. She took the woman's hand, pushed up the sleeve of her gown, and turned her thin arm side to side, examining it. She repeated the same inspection with the other arm. Finally, she lowered the shoulder of the woman's gown and peered closely at the exposed skin.

"Gran? The demon deterrent?" Evangeline motioned toward the corners of the room. "Should I sprinkle the holy water?"

"This isn't the work of a demon."

Evangeline drew closer and gazed down at what it was that had caused Gran's eyes to narrow and her face to cloud over.

There on Mrs. Midsomer's shoulder were two short jagged marks, now puckered white and well on their way to healing, barely visible to the naked eye, certainly invisible to the untrained eye. Something had punctured Mrs. Midsomer's flesh weeks ago, no doubt shortly before her illness began.

Mrs. Midsomer's head snapped backward, and her muscles trembled. Her body erupted into a violent, wracking seizure. Spittle and foam seeped from the corners of her mouth.

While Gran administered drops of owl egg tonic, Evangeline snatched a blue velvet ribbon from her satchel. She tied it around the wrist of the woman's fluttering hand, then dropped to her knees and set an iron nail underneath the bed, doing what she could to keep any other evil spirits at bay.

"No need to bother with that. There are no evil spirits in this room." Gran set the tonic aside and wiped the corners of Mrs. Midsomer's mouth. Her convulsions had eased, but her eyes raced back and forth beneath her closed eyelids. Gran pulled out a fresh cloth, along with a bottle of salt water. She sighed wearily. "We have a long night ahead of us." She set about bathing their patient's face and hands with the salty water.

Of all the unearthly cases Evangeline had assisted Gran with, none had shaken her as much as this one. Maybe it was because they were dealing with someone's mama. Someone's mama who was at a very real risk of dying. Evangeline looked at the family photo on the dresser, and a pang stabbed her heart. She knew what it meant to be without a mama. And, as annoying as Julian had been, she decided she wouldn't be quite so terse the next time she saw him. A Gran lesson came to her: *Everyone has burdens and troubles. Some folks just hold theirs inside better. Others let them out in the form of anger or other sorts of unpleasantness.*

From somewhere in the distance, in the darkness of the humid New Orleans night, a canine howl rose, piercing the air and seeming to seep through the very walls of the house.

Gran glanced toward the window, a shadow of fear creeping across her face.

The blood drained from Evangeline's limbs. In all her years, she had never, not once, seen even a flit of fear cross Gran's features. Worry, yes, but never fear. She'd never known Gran to be afraid of anything.

"What is it, Gran? What's got ahold of her?" Terror squeezed Evangeline by the throat, and for a moment, she couldn't breathe.

Gran's frightened brown eyes met Evangeline's.

"Gran?" Evangeline's voice trembled.

"Rougarou," Gran whispered. "We're dealing with a rougarou."

A rougarou.

Evangeline's legs threatened to buckle, and she clutched one of the bedposts for support. "But the full moon won't rise until tomorrow night. The only rougarou who can morph on the night before or after a full moon is . . ."

"An alpha," Gran finished her sentence for her. She cast another worried glance at the window, as though she could see into the distance beyond it. "And if he's an alpha, his pack is most likely nearby."

Evangeline felt sick to her stomach. "Another three or four rougarous in addition to the alpha," she whispered.

Gran's face grew graver. "Some alphas have been known to expand their packs to as many as six. Anything larger would result in too many members to keep under control.

Remember, it's not a rougarou's goal to draw attention to himself and his family. He wants to hunt unhindered. He wants to be the hunter, not the hunted." She withdrew two handfuls of dried red beans from her pocket. "But first things first." She murmured a blessing over the beans, then poured them into Evangeline's palms. "Place thirteen of these at the doorway and thirteen on each windowsill in this room." She reached into her valise and took out a bulb and tassel perfume bottle filled with yellow liquid.

Evangeline recognized its contents as the blinding venom of the Acadian fang worm. "Do you think it was a rougarou that killed the New Orleanian haunt huntress?"

Gran pressed her lips into a straight line. "I do." She set the bottle on the nightstand within easy reach, should a rougarou gain entrance into the room anyway. She then took a seat beside Mrs. Midsomer, whose breaths were again coming in short, agitated pants. She swabbed the woman's feverish flesh with the saltwater cloth.

Her fingers trembling, Evangeline counted out thirteen beans and lined them up on a window ledge. She hesitated for a moment, dreading what Gran's answer might be, then asked, "Can we help her, Gran?"

"I'm not sure." Gran sat back and sighed. "I'm just not sure. Tell me what you know."

Evangeline finished setting out the rougarou-repelling

blessed beans. She joined Gran at the bedside and recalled what it was Gran had taught her about rougarous, lessons that'd seared themselves into her brain as well as her heart. She didn't believe in hate, but the rougarou was one creature she truly despised, right down to the deepest depths of her soul. Vicious. Heartless. Senseless in their destruction.

A rougarou had stolen her mama's life, and that kind of hate was hard to extinguish.

But there was a job to be done. She pushed the dark thoughts aside. *Focus, Evangeline. Hate blinds.* She took a deep breath. "Only an alpha can infect a victim. Mrs. Midsomer must have been bitten by an alpha on the night of the last full moon. Since then, she's been in the throes of change as her body prepares for the metamorphosis that will occur"—she swallowed hard, her throat suddenly dirt dry—"the metamorphosis that will occur with tomorrow night's full moon."

"Continue." Gran nodded.

"At the first stroke of midnight tomorrow night, her physical transformation will begin, turning her into a mindless, flesh-tearing, bipedal wolf, incapable of resisting her rougarou killer instincts."

"And if she makes a human kill?" Gran prompted.

"But maybe she won't, Gran. If we can prevent it, she'll be miserable for sure. She might even gravely injure herself in her desperation to attack and draw blood, but—"

"Of course we'll try to prevent it," Gran interrupted, "but if despite our best efforts, she succeeds in making a human kill . . ."

Panic leaped inside Evangeline, nearly paralyzing her with a white-hot sense of helplessness. She shook her head, mentally begging Gran not to force her to say more.

"Evangeline?" Gran's mouth was set firmly.

Evangeline took a shuddering breath. "If she makes a human kill tomorrow night, the metamorphosis will be set. And every full moon thereafter, she'll transform into a rampaging beast of teeth and claws, filled with an overpowering taste for blood." She twisted her hands together. "Oh, Gran, what are we going to do?"

"If she makes a kill, you know what we'll have to do." Gran's unwavering gaze was fixed on Evangeline.

"No, Gran," Evangeline whispered.

"We can't knowingly let a rougarou run loose. If we can't discover the alpha and destroy him right away, we'll have no choice, Evangeline. We'll have to destroy her."

Evangeline glanced away, not wanting Gran to see the weakness brimming in her eyes.

"We'll do what we can to keep her comfortable tonight," Gran continued. "Tomorrow evening we'll weaken-bind her and do our best to ease her pain. But when she morphs, if she proves too strong for the holy water–soaked ropes, if she breaks free, it's over."

Gran held out her hand. "Now pass me the infusion of cowslip and frog livers."

The hours passed and they tended to Mrs. Midsomer, patting her burning skin with cooling potions, fending off her muscle spasms and seizures with assorted concoctions.

The foyer clock struck twelve. As it chimed the midnight hour, another wolfish howl sounded in the distance, calling to Mrs. Midsomer. This time, she wailed in return.

Goose bumps raced along Evangeline's neck and arms.

Mrs. Midsomer's eyes fluttered open. No longer the deep blue of a summer sky, they now blazed a fiery green. Evangeline gasped, and the woman turned her eerie gaze upon her, rumbling a low, rabid growl. Evangeline stumbled back, and Mrs. Midsomer gnashed her teeth.

Gran spritzed the air with a vervain mist, causing Mrs. Midsomer to hiss, but her eyes were already returning to their sky-blue color. A trembling took over her body, and her forehead broke out in sweat. Gran blotted Mrs. Midsomer's face dry then held her hand out to Evangeline. "Markers, please."

Evangeline dug through the valise and handed her a package of felt tip pens.

The two of them worked quickly, and when they'd finished drawing a series of multicolored protective symbols, Evangeline packed the pens away.

"The worst is over," Gran murmured. "At least for this night."

Evangeline was not comforted, though. They were certainly going to have their hands full enough taking care of Mrs. Midsomer, but what of the alpha that infected her? What of his pack? They would have to be dealt with, and they'd have to be dealt with soon.

As night faded into dawn, Mrs. Midsomer's symptoms subsided like the passing of a storm. Outside, a catbird chirped in a nearby tree. Evangeline could barely keep her eyes open; they burned with exhaustion, as did every muscle in her body.

Gran dabbed Mrs. Midsomer's forehead with fragrant, calming lilac water, careful not to smudge the protective symbols she and Evangeline had recorded up and down and across her face. With a weary groan, Gran collapsed onto the bedside chair, wincing and rubbing her hip and bad leg.

"You shouldn't have stood on your feet so long," Evangeline chastised. "You should've taken more sit-down breaks."

"Don't worry about me." Gran waved a hand at her.

"I'm tough as an old mule. With a head as hard as one too."

Evangeline was too worn-out to argue. The two of them gazed at Mrs. Midsomer, now resting peacefully.

"She'll sleep soundly through the day," Gran said. "We'll get some rest ourselves. Then we'll prepare the binding ropes and the other provisions we'll need for tonight."

The bedroom door swung open, and Camille breezed in. "Good morning, ladies!" She carried a tray topped with a glass of water, a covered ceramic dish, and a white linen napkin. "I have Mrs. Midsomer's breakfast." She set the tray on the dresser. When she turned toward the sleeping woman, she gasped. "What have you done to her face?" She snatched the napkin and dipped it into the glass of water. "Oh, he won't like this at all," she muttered as she set about scrubbing Mrs. Midsomer's cheeks.

Evangeline couldn't imagine Mr. Midsomer would be all that upset. Maybe a little shocked, but he'd said she and Gran were his last hope, and sadly, he was right. He surely wouldn't question such a harmless preventative measure.

"It's only washable marker," Gran said. "It's not permanent."

Seeming to collect herself, Camille offered them a smile, then shooed them toward the door. "Go on. Go get some rest. The two of you've had a long night."

As Gran packed her valise, Evangeline plucked up the

few white rose petals that had dropped from the bouquet atop the dresser, being mindful not to grasp any of the stems themselves. If a petal were to fall while she was holding one of the roses, it'd be a clear omen of death. She reached into her satchel, pulled out a plastic Baggie, and slipped the velvety pieces into it. They'd come in handy for creating aphrodisiac sachets later.

"There, there, my lady." The maid busied herself wiping off the last of the protection marks from Mrs. Midsomer's cheeks. "Everything's going to be just fine. Camille's here now."

Yawning, Evangeline gathered their bags. As they left, she waved over her shoulder. "Have a good morning, Miss Camille."

They made their way up the staircase, Gran stopping every few steps to rub her leg. Evangeline frowned. The sooner Gran got off her feet, the better.

Inside their room, Evangeline set their bags in the corner, went straight to her bed, and collapsed face-first onto it. Sleep was settling upon her like a warm blanket when a stray thought scuttled by. *Why was Camille so afraid of the docile Mr. Midsomer?* A darker thought followed after it. *Did Mr. Midsomer have a hidden side, a bloodthirsty side with a taste for raw flesh?* Her eyes flew open. He certainly had a taste for raw steak.

A scratching sounded at the door, and Gran let Fader in. He meowed up at her, rubbing circles around her feet and bumping his face into her ankles as she made her way to the bed.

While Gran took a seat and pulled off her work boots, Fader jumped onto the foot of the bed, wrapped his gray tail around himself, and settled down into nap mode.

Evangeline opened her mouth, about to mention her budding suspicion regarding Mr. Midsomer, then thought better of it. Clear thoughts seldom bloomed in exhausted minds. She'd rest on it first. And when she awoke, it might very well prove to be a ridiculous notion.

Yawning, she closed her eyes and fell asleep.

Evangeline dozed for a short while, only to be awakened by the rumblings of her empty stomach.

She sat up, stretching her arms over her head. She glanced at Gran, sound asleep, snoring with one eye open, her face so etched with lines. And that scar. She hadn't ever bothered to question her about that injury either. Evangeline frowned. When all this was over, she'd sit down and ask to hear the story about that. She'd ask to hear all Gran's other stories too. Because now that she thought on it, there was so much about her she didn't know.

Fader, still curled up at Gran's feet, peeled one green eye

open and glared at Evangeline. She stuck her tongue out at him and climbed out of bed.

Now that she'd made a favorable first impression, she no longer needed to wear the awful, itchy dress. She slipped into her jeans and camouflage T-shirt, tucked her mama's talisman inside her collar, then pulled her boots on and fixed her bowie knife to her left leg. She peered into the dresser mirror, pleased to see the calendula salve was doing its work and that she no longer looked like something the cat had dragged in. The shadow croucher's scratch had gone from angry red to shy pink. She unwound the bandage from around her palm and nodded her satisfaction at the pale wound lying there. Her stomach growled again, and she set off to search for breakfast.

The tantalizing smell of coffee and chicory met her at the bottom of the stairs. Another aroma floated alongside it, sweet and sugary.

She followed her nose to the dining room and stopped short at the unexpected sight.

12

Two strange men sat at the table, one burly and bushy browed and uglier than homemade soap, the other handsome and genteel. Mr. Midsomer and Julian, dressed in his school uniform jacket and tie, were seated there too.

"I'm glad to hear next season's float design is on schedule," Mr. Midsomer said from his chair at the head of the table. He was about to speak again when he caught sight of Evangeline standing there. "Oh!" He set down his china coffee cup, and it clinked against the china saucer. "Miss . . . uh . . . Evangeline. Good morning."

"Good morning," she mumbled. She wished the strangers would stop staring at her. Julian paid her no attention whatsoever. He sat hunched over a comic book, completely absorbed in reading, and in eating what looked like little golden-fried pillows blanketed with powdered sugar. A jug of milk, a bottle of chocolate syrup, and a half glass of chocolate milk sat before him.

"John." The handsome and genteel man turned to Mr. Midsomer. "You didn't mention you had houseguests." He smiled pleasantly.

Mr. Midsomer's cheeks colored pink. Evangeline spared him the lie. "I'm one of Mrs. Midsomer's nurses." She started to curtsy but wasn't sure if it was the appropriate response. She did her best to bring up a polite smile instead.

The stranger fixed his dark-blue eyes on her and motioned to the empty chair beside the oblivious Julian. "Join us." He nodded toward the big, scowling man at the other head of the table. "Randall here has brought enough Café Du Monde beignets to feed the entire city of New Orleans. Isn't that right, Randall?"

Randall, who had the build of a heavyweight wrestler and the weatherworn face of a pirate, stared silently at her.

She didn't really want to join them, but the sugary-fried aroma of the doughnut-like pastries drew her like a bear to a beehive. She sat beside Julian, grateful for the full vase of white roses shielding her from the handsome and genteel stranger across the table. He pushed the vase aside and smiled at her. "I didn't catch your name."

"Evangeline." She reached for a beignet, doing her best

to behave in a most mannerly manner that would make Gran proud.

"Evangeline," he repeated, rubbing at the shadow of a beard on his pale-complexioned face. He pursed his delicate lips, then closed his eyes and bowed his head as though trying to recall a lost thought.

Evangeline noticed his brown hair was pulled back in a short ponytail, and she suddenly recognized him as the man who'd driven away from the Midsomers' house yesterday evening in the fancy little convertible.

He glanced back up, steepled his fingers, and spoke. "'Fair was she and young, when in hope began the long journey; Faded was she and old, when in disappointment it ended.'"

Evangeline gaped at him in mid–beignet chew.

"A line from Longfellow's epic poem *Evangeline: A Tale of Acadie*."

Her thoughts dried completely up. She had no idea how to respond.

He gave her a slight grin of embarrassment. "I have a passion for classic literature, as well as French history. Longfellow's poem combines the best of both worlds."

Mr. Midsomer cleared his throat. "Evangeline, these are my uh . . . associates."

"We're krewe members," the ponytailed man explained.

"The krewe is like family to me. I don't have any parents or children, not even a wife, at least not yet. Perhaps there's still hope for me, though." He gave her a friendly wink. "Family is the most important thing there is. Don't you agree?"

Evangeline did indeed agree.

Mr. Midsomer motioned toward the man. "This is the multitalented Mr. Laurent Ardeas. In addition to knowing classic literature and French history, he's also an expert on Greek mythology and is an accomplished thespian, herbalist, genealogist, and I don't know what else."

Laurent Ardeas waved away the words of praise, keeping his eyes on Evangeline. "Please. Call me Laurent."

Mr. Midsomer nodded toward the silent, scowling man at the other end of the table. "This is Mr. Randall Lowell."

The dark-eyed man grunted a greeting.

"Oh, good morning, Miss Evangeline." Camille bustled into the dining room carrying a pot of coffee with her, its fresh-brewed aroma wafting over to meet Evangeline's nose. "I'll bring you a plate and a glass." She refilled Mr. Midsomer's cup and returned a moment later, setting a glass and a china plate before Evangeline. She filled the glass with milk. "Chocolate syrup?"

"Yes, please," Evangeline murmured, very much preferring a cup of coffee instead, but not wanting to make more work for Camille.

Camille topped off Julian's glass then added a squirt of syrup for each of them.

"Excuse me." Julian looked up from his comic book. "Camille, I believe there's been some sort of oversight. This is not my chocolate milk spoon." He held up the stainless steel utensil that had been sitting alongside his china plate. "This is not my antique English silver teaspoon with the mother-of-pearl handle, the one my mother gave me that I specifically use to mix my chocolate milk."

"Now, that spoon you have there will stir your milk just as well." Camille gave him a patient smile.

"But this isn't my chocolate milk spoon," Julian repeated.

Oh, for goodness' sakes, Evangeline wanted to blurt out. Instead, she glanced over at Camille and rolled her eyes.

"It's out in the kitchen with the rest of the silver. Today's polishing day." Camille gave Julian a pat on the head. "I'll bring you your special spoon in a few minutes, as soon as I'm done cleaning it."

Randall Lowell pushed his chair back and climbed to his big feet.

"Well, it seems we must be leaving." Laurent stood and plucked a long-stemmed white rose from the vase. He gave it a sniff with his slightly large nose and handed it across the table to her.

Not wanting to appear rude, she took it.

"A wish for your good health. That's what the white rose symbolizes: good health."

He was wrong. That wasn't the correct meaning at all. White roses were given in recognition of new beginnings, as expressions of hope for the future. That's why they were often used in wedding bouquets. But she couldn't tell him that. Gran would have given her a sour frown for even entertaining the notion of correcting him. "Thank you," she mumbled.

Leaving their coffee and beignets untouched, the men shook Mr. Midsomer's hand. He escorted them to the front door, chatting politely along the way.

Evangeline relaxed, relieved to see them leave, even if it left only her and Julian at the table. She returned the rose to the crystal vase.

With his eyes focused on his comic book, Julian continued chewing and reading.

"Good morning, Julian," she said, unable to keep the trace of disapproval from her tone. Recalling the fate of his mama lying in the room just down the hall, a flood of shame washed over her. She summoned the brightest voice she could and continued, "I'm happy to report your mama is doing well this morning."

Julian nodded, his sight never leaving the pages of his book.

She narrowed her eyes. Why didn't this boy care about his mama? It was almost as though he didn't mind she was in such a bad way. Could he somehow have been responsible for her attack? It was a crazy thought, and Evangeline started to shoo it away, then paused, studying him a little closer. He was smart, that was for sure. But was it possible he was some sort of heartless, evil genius?

"He owns a chain of floral shops," Julian muttered, startling her. He was still reading his comic book.

"What?"

"Laurent Ardeas. He owns a chain of flower stores, and an antique furniture shop, and a bunch of other local businesses. He's always bringing white roses. Randall Lowell always brings food. Some of the others bring get-well cards and small gifts." He shrugged. "That's what people do when someone is sick." He kept reading.

Evangeline nodded. The folks back home would do the same if she or Gran were ever bedridden. "Do they work on a boat with your daddy?"

Julian looked up, his eyebrows squishing together. "My father doesn't work on a boat."

"But Mr. Ardeas said they were crew members. I thought—"

"*Krewe* members, with a *k*. Not *crew* with a *c*. They're part of the Krewe of Circe, a Mardi Gras social club, a brotherhood of sorts. Laurent founded the group a couple of years ago and invited my father to ride with them this past season."

"Oh." Evangeline's cheeks warmed with a tinge of embarrassment.

Reading her expression as one of confusion, Julian set his comic book down and folded his hands on the tabletop. "While there are many parades rolling throughout the Mardi Gras season, Mardi Gras day itself is a daylong celebration of parades and revelry occurring on the Tuesday before Ash Wednesday—the day on which Catholics repent of their sins by having a priest ceremonially mark their foreheads with ashes in—"

"I know what Mardi Gras is, for goodness' sakes, even if I've never been to a New Orleans one." Evangeline crossed her arms. "And I am most certainly knowledgeable about Catholicism. A haunt huntress is well versed in all forms of faiths—" She stopped herself, resisting the urge to glare at him for causing her to spill more information about her and Gran.

"You shouldn't feel embarrassed about your hobby." He picked up his comic book and resumed reading it.

"Hobby?" Evangeline clenched her fists and narrowed her eyes.

"I enjoy constructing models of medieval siege weaponry, most specifically trebuchets, catapults, and ballistas, though I abhor violence. The sight of people engaging in physical combat severely elevates my anxiety levels, sometimes causing me to vomit." He turned a page of his book. "I recently completed construction of a marble-shooting crossbow. My mother says I possess a keen talent for design." The corners of his mouth turned down, and his eyes took on a sad, faraway look.

Camille strode into the dining room carrying the gleaming silver tea service before her. She set it down on the mahogany buffet, then pulled a pearl-handled silver teaspoon from her apron pocket and held it up to Julian with a smile. "Now it's all nice and shiny." She placed it beside his glass of milk and returned a moment later with an armful of silver pitchers and vases glinting beneath the light of the crystal chandelier. Humming to herself, she arranged them in their proper places behind the glass doors of the antique china cabinet. On her way out she paused, squinted at the silver teapot, then pulled a cloth from her pocket. After giving the shiny surface a quick buff, she resumed her humming and headed back to the kitchen.

Frowning, Julian watched her go. "She just polished the silver a few days ago." He shook his head. "I fear she may be going a bit overboard with her housekeeping duties."

A horn tooted outside.

"Julian!" Mr. Midsomer called from the foyer. "Your ride's here."

"Excuse me." Julian closed the cover of his comic book and set it on the table. He wiped the powdered sugar from his mouth and fingers with his linen napkin, brushed a beignet crumb from the lapel of his school uniform jacket, then left.

Evangeline watched as Julian straightened his tie, grabbed his backpack, and headed toward the front door. She'd been wrong to suspect him of any misdeeds. Just the mention of his mama a moment ago nearly made him go teary eyed.

She shoved half a beignet into her mouth. Her gaze fell upon Julian's comic book, and the sugary doughnut seemed to turn to concrete in her mouth. She swallowed hard. There on the cover, a wild-eyed, snarling man stared out. Long, silver knife-like claws protruded from his knuckles. She didn't have to read the pages to know he was a superhero character with killer wolf-like powers. Did Julian see wolves as heroes? Would he want his mama to become one? Was his daddy already one? Did he hope to become one too, making them all one happy rougarou family?

No. She shook her head. Mr. Midsomer was heartbroken over his wife's condition. And he was the one who'd brought her and Gran here to help. She was being ridiculous. Too much worrying and not enough resting would do that to a person.

Evangeline and Gran spent the rest of the morning preparing an assortment of potions and poultices. Then they cut some rope into the appropriate lengths and converted them into weakening binds through the application of holy water and prayer.

They were still working on preparations when a knock sounded.

"Come in," Gran called.

Camille opened the bedroom door, a cleaning rag in one hand, a bottle of polish in the other. "Mr. Midsomer brought some po'boy sandwiches from the corner grocery."

"Thank you, Camille," Gran answered. "We'll be down in a moment."

Camille gave them a parting nod, then turned and clicked the door shut behind her.

Eager to get to lunch, Evangeline quickly threaded the last pearl onto a madness-prevention bracelet, while Gran finished filling a potpourri bag with the evil-repelling ingredient of crushed bay leaves.

As they made their way down to the dining room, Gran focused on gripping the staircase banister. Evangeline focused on the sandwiches, her mouth watering. She hoped Mr. Midsomer had brought fried shrimp po'boys rather than roast beef or hot sausage. But when they reached the ground floor and Gran released the railing, her foot shot out from under her. Her arms pinwheeled, and she crashed to the hardwood floor with a thump and a cry as her cane clattered away.

"Gran!" Evangeline rushed to her, she too nearly slipping on the slick wooden surface.

Gran lay on her side, her bad leg jutting out at an unnatural angle.

Evangeline knelt beside her, doing her best to assess the situation, but it didn't take special skill to comprehend Gran was in a bad way.

"Oh, dear!" Camille hurried over, her eyes wide, her hands pressed to the sides of her face. "Oh, Mrs. Holyfield, are you okay?"

Wincing, Gran struggled to sit up, her face pinched with pain.

"Oh, goodness gracious! How foolish of me, how foolish of me." Camille wrung her hands. "I forgot all about your frail condition, Mrs. Holyfield. I just wasn't thinking at all when I waxed the floor."

By then Mr. Midsomer had joined them. He knelt beside Gran, took one look at her crooked leg, and grimaced.

"Gran, let me help you up." Evangeline grasped her by the hand.

But Mr. Midsomer shook his head, his brow creased with worry. "I fear her leg might be broken. I think we need to call an ambulance."

Fader came galloping up the hallway and straight toward Gran. He rubbed back and forth against her and butted his head into her arm. Then he sat down beside her and gave a loud, piteous yowl.

13

Evangeline's conscious mind blurred, muddying like water lapping the bank of the bayou. While Camille and Mr. Midsomer did what they could to keep Gran comfortable until the paramedics arrived, Evangeline raced upstairs. She hurried around the room, packing her satchel with a long length of string, a stone with a naturally occurring hole bored through its center, and a spray bottle filled with an infusion of elder leaves collected on the eve of May Day. She slipped the bag over her shoulder, then dug to the bottom of Gran's valise and pulled out a vial containing a mixture of powdered moss, henbane, and vinegar.

Uncorking the vial as she went, she rushed downstairs and gently dabbed the injury-soothing mixture onto Gran's broken leg while chanting a healing spell.

Neither she nor Gran protested when the paramedics arrived, loaded Gran onto a stretcher, and slid her into the back of the ambulance. They both knew her injury was far too severe for a haunt huntress's type of healing. They knew it would take the skills of a surgeon to piece her broken bone together again.

The hours ticked past in the hospital waiting room.

Finally Mr. Midsomer rose from his seat. "Would you like anything? A soda? Some coffee?"

Evangeline shook her head.

"Try not to worry. Your grandmother's going to be fine."

Evangeline didn't reply.

"I understand what you're feeling." Mr. Midsomer swallowed hard, his voice dropping to little more than a whisper. "My wife and my son are everything to me."

Evangeline cast a glance up at him, reading the truth of his words on his sad face. He really did love his wife, and even though he might not understand Julian, he did love him.

Mr. Midsomer cleared his throat. "I'll tell you what. The hospital president is a friend of mine, a fellow krewe member. How about I go speak with him, ask him to make sure your grandmother will be well taken care of?"

"Thank you, Mr. Midsomer." Evangeline returned her

gaze downward. Her fingers worked at the long piece of string she'd packed in her satchel, tying knots in it and creating a cordon to loop around Gran's wrist to promote rapid healing. Her mind worked on knotting itself with worry. She tried hard not to think of the grim waiting to escort Gran to the other side. Losing her mama had cut a hole in her heart. To have Gran die and create another such hole would leave her as hollow and fragile as a dried-out honeycomb.

It might have been a half hour later, maybe longer, Evangeline had lost track of time, when Mr. Midsomer returned. A doctor in a white lab coat arrived with him, along with a portly gentleman wearing a business suit and a bushy walrus moustache.

"Evangeline, this is Dr. Guidry." Mr. Midsomer motioned to the man in the lab coat. "He'll be taking care of your grandmother." He motioned to the man in the suit. "This is Mr. Woolsey, the friend I was telling you about. He's the hospital's president."

Mr. Woolsey extended his large hand to Evangeline. She took it and shook. His grip was strong, his fingers cold. "John here has filled me in on the situation," he announced with a booming voice. "You can rest assured, young lady. Your dear grandmother will receive the very best of care this institution has to offer. You can depend on G. B. Woolsey."

"Thank you, sir." Evangeline's voice sounded weak and pathetic in her ears.

Dr. Guidry spoke next, brief and businesslike as he addressed Evangeline. He spoke of the previous fracture to Gran's femur, the large bone that ran from her hip to her knee. Surgery would be required. It had to be done, or the consequences would be dire. She could visit with her grandmother first if she'd like, just for a few minutes before they took her to surgery.

Evangeline's mind went blurry again, and she murmured her thanks as the doctor and Mr. Woolsey left the room.

"Evangeline?" Mr. Midsomer's brow furrowed. "Evangeline, are you okay?"

"Yes." She nodded. "Yes. I'm just fine," she lied.

He glanced at his watch. "I apologize, but I really must leave. I have a previous work commitment. Don't worry." He started to pat her head, then stopped and drew his hand away. "Your grandmother's in very good hands."

"Thank you." Evangeline nodded numbly.

Mr. Midsomer gave her directions back to the house, which was only a four-block walk, and then he was gone.

A nurse came to escort her to Gran's room. Evangeline followed, the surroundings blurring as they made their way up the wide, brightly lit hallway, past patients in squeaky wheelchairs, past the cafeteria smelling of onion soup, past an area cordoned off with fluorescent yellow tape and bustling with construction workers. A large sign had been posted to the nearby wall announcing the addition of the hospital's new fitness center, thanks to a generous contribution from local businessman Laurent Ardeas.

Mr. Woolsey stood in the midst of the activity, nodding vigorously and booming into his phone, "Yes, Laurent. All the plans are in place. You can depend on G. B. Woolsey. Every detail has been attended to, and congratulations will soon be in order."

They entered through a set of double doors and turned a few more corners, and the nurse came to a stop at the end of a long hallway. "Here we are." She opened the room door, motioned Evangeline to step inside, then set off to attend to her other duties.

"Evangeline," Gran murmured. Her scarred face looked older, so tired and frail.

An ember of guilt burned inside Evangeline. If she had gained her haunt huntress status by now, she would be the one hunting monsters. Gran could be retired, sitting in her rocking chair back home instead of lying in a hospital bed here. She took the spray bottle from her satchel and spritzed the air with the elder leaf infusion to aid Gran with the process of healing.

Gran motioned her to come closer. "You must get back to the swamp. Call Percy to come fetch you and Fader. There's no time to send a cardinal; use the telephone." She pointed to the beige-colored phone on the bedside table that was just out of her reach. "Gather our things from the Midsomer house and leave as quickly as you can. You're in danger here, and I can't protect you while confined to this hospital bed."

Evangeline felt around inside her satchel and pulled out the holed stone potent with special healing properties. She tucked it beneath Gran's pillow. "Gran. I can protect myself."

"Listen, and don't interrupt. Get Julian and Mr. Midsomer out of the house. Secure Mrs. Midsomer with the weaken-binds. Place protections all around her room. It's the best we can do for her. Then you must leave with Percy. You mustn't be anywhere near Mrs. Midsomer when the midnight hour arrives."

But Evangeline wasn't afraid. She had been training for this moment all her life. Her heart warmed with pride. "Gran." She stroked her grandmama's lined forehead. "I might not be an official haunt huntress yet, but I was born to a haunt huntress and raised by one of the best. I can't turn my back on this family. I have a job to do."

Gran squeezed her eyes shut. For a moment, Evangeline

feared she'd been overcome by the pain in her broken leg, but when Gran opened her eyes, they were filled with sadness, and strangely enough, shame.

"Evangeline, there's something I need to tell you." She paused, seeming to search for the right words. "I've kept things from you. Maybe I shouldn't have. Raising a child is the hardest job in the world, far harder than hunting monsters. There're so many questions, so many directions to take, and the right way is never clear." She took a deep breath and let it out slowly. "I did what I thought was best. I guess time will tell if I was right."

"Gran?" Evangeline's pulse thudded. She didn't like the direction this conversation was heading.

"We weren't assigned this New Orleans job. I volunteered for it."

Evangeline already knew that much. A needle of guilt jabbed at her conscience for having read Gran's letter from the council.

"It's a job that was personal to me—and to you—a job I thought I'd finished nearly thirteen years ago. But I was wrong."

The door opened, and a nurse came in. She checked the bag of IV fluid hanging on a pole beside the bed. She turned to Evangeline. "I'm afraid you'll have to leave now. We'll be prepping Mrs. Holyfield for surgery soon."

Gran lifted her index finger. "Just a moment longer, please."

The nurse frowned. "All right. But only a few more minutes." She turned and left, her white shoes squeaking against the linoleum floor. The door clicked shut after her.

"Back then, we had a dangerous rougarou situation on our hands," Gran continued. "An alpha had taken up residence in the swamp. He'd already infected four men, and word was he planned to expand his pack even more, maybe even add a mate. The council had no choice but to call a meeting to devise a way to destroy him. But we were betrayed. One of their human familiars told the monster what we were planning." She paused and fixed an eye on Evangeline. "You know all about their human familiars and how to identify them, right?"

"Yes, ma'am." Evangeline recited from memory. "The human familiar serves as an attendant to his rougarou master, not only providing physical protection but also functioning as a spy and confidant. The rougarou's familiar can be identified by the two small tattoos worn on the inner wrist: those of a black fang and a single red droplet."

Gran nodded. She paused for another moment, then gave a sad sigh. "Your mama was making her way to our gathering that night when she was ambushed by one of their familiars." The corners of her mouth turned down and her voice dropped. "The familiar tore off your mama's silver talisman and flung it away, and that's when the alpha attacked her."

Evangeline's head went light, but her limbs seemed to suddenly fill with lead. Gran had never revealed this particular information to her before. She touched her mama's talisman hanging around her neck, hoping to draw comfort from it, but her eyes welled up anyway.

Gran drew a shaky breath. "After the attack, his human pack members marched into our meeting, dragging your injured mama after them." Gran swallowed hard. "They threw her and her dying familiar to the floor. They ordered us to cease our plans to destroy their alpha and their family. Then they left, warning they'd strike again, killing more haunt huntresses if necessary."

Gran's lip trembled. "Her injuries were so severe. We tried to save her and the baby, but we couldn't." Tears filled her eyes.

"But Gran." Evangeline grabbed her by her warm hand. "You did save her baby. I'm right here."

Gran shook her head. "That baby was born dead. She's buried in the same coffin with your mama in St. Petite's churchyard."

The world slipped out from under Evangeline. Black dots danced before her eyes. "Gran," she whispered again,

"I'm right here. I'm not dead and buried. I'm not a ghost."
It must be the pain medicine. She glanced at the half-empty
IV bag. It must be fogging Gran's mind, making her talk
nonsense. But Gran's eyes, though filled with sorrow, were
as clear as ever.

Gran fiddled with the bed covers. "We chanted. We
applied poultices. Your mama took my hand, and she said
to me, 'Tell little Percy and his daddy they will always have
my love. No time or space can sever it.'" The tears now
rolled freely down Gran's wrinkled cheeks. "She used what
little life force she had left to speak her final words, 'I know
you'll raise her up right and train her to be the best haunt
huntress Louisiana has ever known. Her name is to be
Matilde Evangeline Clement.' Then she slipped away, her
spirit vanishing like a butterfly made of light, extinguished
in the world's wide darkness." Gran squeezed her eyes shut,
suffering a pain more unbearable than a hundred splintered
femurs.

Evangeline tried to swallow but couldn't, nor could she
breathe. Either Gran had lost her mind, or she was not who
she'd thought herself to be all these years.

Gran wasn't finished, though. She sighed heavily. "Her
lifeless daughter was born shortly after. I held her in my
hands, and I proclaimed her name Matilde, but that's as far
as I got." Gran wiped her tears and smiled. A flicker of joy

sparked in her brown eyes.

If Evangeline had been questioning the stability of Gran's sanity a moment ago, she was now convinced it'd completely taken flight and left the building.

"But like green shoots fighting their way through a fire-swept forest floor, there amid the deepest sorrow of my life was born one of my greatest joys. Matilde was taken from my hands, so I could receive her sister into them. Oh, she was smaller, downright puny, but she had a mighty powerful set of lungs, and oh, was she sassy. I loved her more than my own life at the first sight of her." Gran squeezed Evangeline's hand, then rested the back of it against her weathered cheek.

"Gran?" Evangeline whispered. "What are you saying?"

Fresh tears brimmed in Gran's eyes, and she nodded. "It hasn't happened often over the past two hundred years, but it's not unheard of for a haunt huntress to give birth to twin daughters."

"But . . ." Evangeline's tongue was as tied as her tangled thoughts.

"Because a haunt huntress must choose the name for her daughter, and since your sister had been bestowed with the first one, that left the second one for you. So I proclaimed you Evangeline Clement."

For a moment, the world ceased to exist. Only a blinding

white wall of shock and confusion surrounded Evangeline. A sister? She'd had . . . a twin sister? "Gran . . . why didn't you tell me?" She swallowed hard. "Why'd you keep it secret all this time?"

"I'm sorry, Evangeline. Honestly. I am." Gran sighed. "I watched your struggles and your self-doubts over the years. I knew you felt adrift without your mama. I didn't want any of it to affect your development as a haunt huntress. It's when we start to believe our doubts that we fail at the things at which we should succeed."

Evangeline had so many questions, her mind twisted and flipped like a catfish in a net. What would her name have been had her sister lived? Would they look exactly alike? Would they think the same way, like the same things? Would they have the same interests? But most important, would they both have inherited the haunt huntress talent and powers?

She fixed her eyes on Gran's. She didn't want to ask, she didn't want to hear the answer. Yet it was the only answer that mattered in all the world. "Gran . . . am I a haunt huntress? Or am I a middling?"

The smile slipped from Gran's face, and Evangeline's innards iced over.

Gran shook her head. "I don't know."

Evangeline's knees buckled. She pulled a chair over and collapsed onto it. "Tell it to me straight, Gran. No sugarcoating. I can handle it." She wasn't really sure she could handle it, but she was determined to maintain her dignity and composure as Gran had taught her a good haunt huntress always should.

"Very well." Gran gave her a somber, understanding nod. "There are three possibilities." She held up her index finger. "One. You and your sister each inherited full haunt huntress powers. But such a situation has occurred only once."

Whatever foundation of hope Evangeline had managed to retain now crumbled beneath her.

Gran held up a second finger. "Two. You and your sister inherited the powers, but split the amount between you, fifty percent going to each of you."

Gran paused, pressing her lips together for a moment. "Or"—she slowly lifted a third finger—"it's possible one girl received all the powers, and the other received none. In which case, the girl who received none would be considered a middling."

"I see." Evangeline glanced down, disappointed, ashamed, and having no idea who she was. Did she have full powers? Half? Or, was she empty, the end of Gran's long, unbroken line of haunt huntress ancestors. Considering she was almost thirteen and a familiar had not yet made itself known to her . . . Well, there was her answer, the answer she'd been fearing but had known in her heart all along. There was no denying it any longer. She was a middling. She swallowed, forcing away the lump burning in back of her throat.

"Evangeline, I don't know what amount of powers you have, but I do know you're something very special. I see it in you, even if you don't."

Evangeline had never felt more powerless in all her life. She stared down at the floor.

"I know becoming a haunt huntress is what you've dreamed of all your life." Gran scrutinized Evangeline's face, reading the doubt there as clearly as reading the rain in a swollen gray cloud. "Oh, Evangeline." Gran took her by the hand and gave it a tender squeeze. "This isn't the end of your path. I don't know which direction you're headed or where you'll end up, but I *can* tell you this: your journey's only just beginning. Evangeline, Look at me."

Evangeline met Gran's eyes.

"Power comes from belief. If you don't believe you have it, then you don't. But if you believe in yourself, amazing things will happen."

As far as Evangeline was concerned, those were just fluffy words. They had no weight or heft. If Gran really believed in her, she wouldn't be asking her to flee from this job.

"A young haunt huntress has no business going up against a rougarou on her own," Gran said as though reading her mind. "A rougarou is inhumanly strong and completely heartless. You must get yourself to safety."

What other choice did she have? Evangeline nodded.

Gran arched an eyebrow, evidently believing she needed further convincing. "On that night when you were born, I left you in the care of the council members and went after the alpha on my own. Part of me wanted to protect innocent people, but another part, and it shames me to confess it, wanted to exact revenge, which is not the haunt huntress way.

"I hadn't gotten far into the swamp when the alpha jumped down from the branch of an oak and attacked me. Despite the blistering burns my talisman gave him, he still slashed at my face."

"Gran." Evangeline shook her head. "You've already relived too many painful memories. You can tell me the rest later."

Gran shook her head back at Evangeline. "You need to hear this. I still had enough fury and strength to fuel me. I fought with everything I had. And so did he. He nearly tore my leg away."

"Your leg," Evangeline whispered, glancing down at Gran's newly rebroken limb. Then she touched the faded scar running down the side of Gran's face. "It was the alpha. He did this to you."

Gran nodded. "When he decided I'd had enough, he left. He'd made his point. I was no longer a threat."

Evangeline's ears buzzed, and her stomach flipped upside down. She didn't want to hear any more.

Gran sighed. "It'd have been better if he'd left me for dead. But he left me for worse. The only humans who survive an alpha's attack are the ones he *wants* to survive, ensuring that at the next full moon, that person will transform into one of the same foul and hellish creatures."

Gran was certainly capable of keeping big secrets, but Evangeline was pretty sure being a rougarou wasn't one of them. If that alpha was still alive, Gran would be morphing into a vicious, snarling, fur-covered beast every month. "You killed him. You killed the alpha."

"I did." Gran nodded.

A spark of pride flared inside Evangeline as she pieced the scene together. "You let him believe you'd been defeated, that he'd whipped all the fight out of you. But when he walked away, you got him."

Gran nodded again. "Climbed up onto my good leg and shot him through the heart with a silver bullet from my pearl-grip derringer, the one I kept strapped to my leg and hidden just beneath my skirt." She fixed an eye on Evangeline. "I took a chance and won. It cost me a lot, but I was willing to pay higher. If I'd failed, he not only would have slain the council, he'd have gone after you too." She shrugged as though it had all been in a day's work. "Killing the alpha broke his blood hold, changing his pack members back into men. They and their human familiars scattered like cockroaches and hightailed it out of town. Since then, there's been no sight or sound of a rougarou anywhere near. Until now."

"But Gran, what are we, I mean, what are you and the council going to do about the alpha who's out there now?"

"You and I," Gran said, "will go back home, and with the help of the council, we'll figure something out."

Three knocks sounded, and Evangeline jumped.

The nurse stepped into the room. As she replaced the nearly empty IV bag with a fresh one, she fixed her firm gaze on Evangeline. "I'm afraid visiting time's over. Doctor's orders." She patted Gran's arm. "Mrs. Holyfield's going to take a nap now."

"I'm not tired."

"You will be," the nurse looked at her watch, "in ten seconds."

Gran glanced at the IV bag, then glared at the nurse. "What did you put in there?"

The nurse smiled sweetly. "Doctor's orders."

Gran's head slumped to the side, and one eye went droopy. "Evangeline. Promise me you'll . . ."

"Gran!" Evangeline sprang up, her heart slamming inside her chest.

"It's okay," the nurse reassured her. "It's just a harmless sedative. A little something to relax her before surgery."

Gran's one eye fell shut. The other stared out straight ahead. Frowning, the nurse reached over to close the eyelid, but Evangeline blocked her hand. "No. That's the way she sleeps."

"O-kay." The nurse moved toward the door. "And now

you really must leave."

Evangeline looped the knotted cordon around Gran's wrist, then leaned down and kissed her on her scarred cheek. "Don't worry, Gran. Fader and I will get back home. And you'll be safe here." She went to give Gran's talisman a reassuring pat, but it wasn't there. She yanked down the thin blanket. There was no silver talisman lying against Gran's hospital gown. She whirled around on the nurse. "Gran's talisman! Where is it?"

"Now, don't worry." The nurse extended her hands in a *just-simmer-down* motion. "Per hospital policy, patients aren't allowed to wear jewelry. We'll keep her necklace safe until she's discharged."

"Oh." Evangeline drew the blanket back up to Gran's chin. "Okay . . . I guess." But she did not like this hospital policy at all.

The nurse pulled the door open and motioned for her to leave.

Evangeline's heart drooped like a wet rag that'd been squeezed and wrung out. She wanted to cry, but she did not. She straightened her back, held her head high, and left.

She stood in the cold hallway, the heaviness of Gran's confession pressing down on her as though she were standing at the bottom of the ocean. Visitors and staff flowed past like schools of fish, but she'd never felt so alone in her life. Her mama was gone. Her sister was gone. Her hopes and self-worth, her future as a haunt huntress—vanished. And if the hateful grim had its way, Gran would be leaving her too. She forced her booted feet to move and made her way to the hospital's tiny chapel.

Holy sanctuaries were her place of comfort, their quiet peacefulness always putting into perspective whatever was troubling her. She knelt before the altar scattered with flickering candles in glass jars. Willing herself to shut out her anguish, at least for the moment, she murmured a prayer for Gran's safekeeping and for that of Mrs. Midsomer. She prayed for the strength to accept things as they were, then quieted her mind even further. Sometimes her troubled heart and soul cleared right away; other times it took a bit longer for comfort to appear.

The only thing to appear to her this time, though, was the remembrance of her itchy knee yesterday morning, the indicator she'd soon be kneeling inside a strange church. And here she was. She'd seen a lot of other signs and portents over the past two days too, all of them dark and unwelcoming. She gazed up at the chapel's stained-glass window, and the breath caught in her throat.

There in vivid reds, greens, blues, and yellows, a wolf was taking a small boy and girl by their hands. Sin leading innocents astray. On the other side of the window, the sun was sinking, steadily drawing the day to its end.

Evangeline leaped up. She had much to do before the arrival of the midnight hour.

Evangeline descended the hospital's front steps, and a gust of wind blew past, whipping around leaves and sending an empty soda can rattling down the street. The weather had picked up since they'd arrived at the hospital that afternoon. The sky now hung gray and swollen.

Her heart as heavy as the clouds overhead, she set off toward the Midsomers' home. As her boot heels clacked hollowly against the sidewalk, a sudden sensation fluttered against the back of her neck, and she stopped.

Someone was watching her.

She whirled around, certain she would come face-to-face with the spy, but no one was there.

Just nerves, she reassured herself. She'd had a bad day, to say the least. Being a bit jumpy was to be expected. She turned and resumed walking.

She would do what Gran had instructed. She would tend to Mrs. Midsomer, evict everyone else from the house, then go back to the swamp. She'd return in shame, not having discovered her familiar, not having proven she had heart, and with not even a spark of haunt huntress magic igniting inside her. She'd return as a middling. But worse than that, she would have abandoned the Midsomer family, tucking tail and running away in their greatest time of need.

At least Gran would be safe. No rougarou would try to attack her in a hospital. And as soon as the doctors said Gran had recovered enough to go home, she and Percy would drive back and retrieve her.

Barely paying attention to her surroundings, she was passing a three-story brick building, its tall windows covered with tightly shut faded green shutters, when a scruffy brown dog lunged from the doorway. The half schnauzer, half mutt perked its ears, splayed its four legs, and unleashed a barrage of barking, startling Evangeline from her thoughts and bringing her feet to a quick stop.

"Mind your manners, Ju-Ju!" a huddled figure called from the doorway. The owner of the voice wore a dirty blanket wrapped around her bony shoulders; a paper shopping bag filled with what Evangeline guessed were her worldly possessions sat beside her on the gray sidewalk.

Ju-Ju wagged his tail at the sound of the woman's voice.

"Hello." Evangeline nodded to the woman. She crouched and petted the little dog as it pranced in place, its claws clicking against the pavement. It erupted into another round of barking.

The woman in the doorway leaned out of her blanket and fixed her eyes on Evangeline's face, her own face as creased with cracks as the broken and bumpy street next to the sidewalk. "Ju-Ju says you carrying a heavy load in your heart."

Evangeline sighed miserably. "Yes, ma'am. That's true." Her heart did indeed weigh a ton.

A brisk breeze whipped by. The woman tilted her head back and sniffed deeply. "This wind ain't normal. There's something in it. Something bad. Ju-Ju smells it too."

Ju-Ju barked his agreement, his tail wagging a hundred miles an hour. He spun around, and a tiny gray bag swung from his dirty red collar.

Evangeline's eye's widened. She didn't have to ask what it was. Gran had taught her all about them. "A gris-gris bag," she whispered. She glanced at the woman, who also wore a small sack hanging from a long leather cord around her neck. Evangeline's heart lightened a few hundred pounds. A gris-gris bag couldn't remove the rougarou's curse from Mrs. Midsomer, but it could provide another layer of protection for her, a little something extra to reinforce the weaken-binds. An ember of hope glowed inside Evangeline. She might not have any haunt huntress magic to offer, but that didn't mean she couldn't use someone else's magic to aid Mrs. Midsomer.

"You best be getting off the streets, girl." The woman in the doorway nodded, then mumbled, "Mmm-hmm," as though confirming the wisdom of her own advice.

"Yes, ma'am." Evangeline indicated the tiny sack hanging from the woman's neck. "I'm in need of a gris-gris bag. . . . It's an emergency situation. Can you point me to the nearest voodoo temple?" Ju-Ju licked the back of her hand. She scratched his ears, and he closed his eyes in canine bliss.

The woman gave her a silent stare. For a moment, Evangeline feared she wouldn't answer, but then she pointed across the street with her crooked finger. "You want Papa Urbain's. Head one block over to Dumaine, then down toward the river."

Another gust of wind whipped by, bringing plastic straws and pigeon feathers skittering up the road.

"Thank you!" Evangeline gave Ju-Ju a final head ruffle, then jumped to her feet and raced away.

"Get off the streets soon, girl!" the woman called after her. "It won't be safe when the sun sets. Evil hides easy in the dark."

Evangeline's gator-skin boots tapped against the dirty sidewalk as she ran. The strange breeze combed through her hair. She wove her way through throngs of tourists laughing and staggering and clutching plastic cups with their contents sloshing over the rims. She sprinted past multistory Spanish Colonial–style shops and homes, their intricate cast-iron balconies draped with leftover Mardi Gras beads and purple, green, and gold bunting. Behind their wrought-iron gates, flagstone alleyways led to hidden courtyards lush with greenery and burbling stone fountains.

A blue neon sign advertising *Readings* hung above the doorway of the squat two-story building. The shop's faded and flaking shutters were in desperate need of a fresh coat of paint. Nearly breathless, Evangeline pushed the creaky door open and entered.

The dimly lit interior hung heavy with the scents of herbs and spicy incense. Carved wooden masks glared down from the deep-red walls. Anyone stepping into the place, even Julian Midsomer himself, would've felt the strong magic there. Altars were stationed everywhere, their surfaces covered with burning candles and assorted odds and ends like coins, oyster shells, wine bottles, and the figurines of Catholic saints, their eyes gazing mournfully at Evangeline.

"Hello?" She glanced around at the counters and shelves

crowded with glass canisters of every dried ingredient one could imagine, as well as a bowl filled with chicken feet dyed purple and blue. A set of doorway curtains at the side of the room parted, and Evangeline whirled around.

A tall man stood in the shadows, the pupils of his dark eyes glinting gold as they reflected the candlelight emanating around the room. After a moment, he spoke quietly, almost reverently, his voice deep and rich. "How can I help you?"

"I'm . . . I'm looking for Papa Urbain," Evangeline murmured, a current of nervousness zinging through her. She was standing on unfamiliar territory. She couldn't afford to say or do the wrong thing. Inadvertently insulting a voodoo priest would not only be poor form, for which Gran would have been very disappointed in her, but she could also end up walking away without a gris-gris bag.

The man stepped from the doorway. The glint fell away from his eyes, and Evangeline released her breath. With his neatly trimmed gray beard and a pair of reading glasses hanging around his neck, he could have passed for a typical suburban grandfather, though he was anything but typical.

"Are you Papa Urbain?"

"I am."

"I'm in need of a gris-gris bag, sir. For a woman. A client."

He didn't reply, waiting instead for her to divulge more specifics.

Evangeline took a deep breath. "The woman was infected by the bite of an alpha rougarou. I was hoping you could provide something to bring her improved health and luck, something that might magnify the efforts of those trying to help her."

Keeping his intense gaze on her, he folded his arms over his chest, a gold ring with a bloodred stone gleaming on his pinky in the flickering flame light. "You're rather young to have such responsibilities as clients."

"Well, she's really more my gran's client." Evangeline resisted the urge to nervously twist her fingers together. "My gran's a haunt huntress, but she's in the hospital right now."

"A haunt huntress. I see. And you?"

Evangeline's face flushed. The cramped, dark shop suddenly grew hotter. "I'm a . . . a . . ." But she couldn't bring herself to say the word. Not that she needed to. The Voodoo priest would be able to see it well enough for himself.

He pulled one of the curtains back on the doorway behind him and motioned for her to enter.

The aroma of incense hung even thicker inside the small temple. A wooden table stood in the room's center; a scuffed counter loomed at the back. Along one wall a single altar had been erected, this one bearing a statuette of Mother Mary along with a bowl of dirt, a lit candle, a stick of burning incense, and a goblet of water: the representations of earth, fire, wind, and water.

The altar had also been set with a scattering of personal items—a hairbrush, a paper fan, a pair of women's sunglasses—objects evidently belonging to a revered ancestor.

A sudden hissing drew Evangeline's attention to the countertop the voodoo priest now stood behind. A fat black pine snake coiling there in a pool of shadows gave her a lazy flick of its forked tongue. On a perch behind the counter sat a white bird, its beak and feet a pale pink color. It stared at her with unblinking blue-gray eyes. Evangeline stared back, easily identifying it as a crow. And though she'd heard of such rare white crows before, she'd never actually seen one.

"That's Beyza." Papa Urbain nodded toward the bird. "She's my eyes and my ears." He reached under the counter and brought forth a leather bag. "She keeps an eye on the things that need keeping an eye on." He drew open the bag, took out a flat seashell, and set it aside. Then he dumped the rest of the contents into his hand. Cupping his palms together, he gave them a shake and dropped the items onto the countertop with a clatter.

Gran's schooling had trained Evangeline well, allowing her to easily recognize the small scattered pieces as possum bones.

Papa Urbain pulled on his reading glasses and frowned

down at the countertop, disturbed by what he saw in the throw. Using the seashell, he moved the bones around, careful not to touch them with his long fingers. He studied them at length, then finally looked up at Evangeline and shook his head sadly. "I'm sorry." He sighed and removed his eyeglasses. "But that is the way of the world."

16

"What? What's the way of the world? What do you see?" Evangeline's heart boomed like summer thunder.

"I see bloodshed associated with your client."

"Bloodshed?" The image of a wolfish Mrs. Midsomer leaped into Evangeline's head. Fear clawed at her chest. Mrs. Midsomer was doomed. The weaken-binds would not work. Come midnight, the rougarou madness would overtake her, and she would make her first kill.

Papa Urban frowned, and he shook his head again, repeating, "I'm sorry."

With a struggle, Evangeline took a shuddering breath. "Well, thank you anyway. If you could still prepare a gris—"

"There's more." White candlelight glowed in the priest's dark eyes. "Death is near you. Two people will die tonight."

His words hit Evangeline like a punch. All feeling drained from her limbs. "Oh," she whispered.

He swept the bones and shell back into the bag. "As you know, I cannot reverse the rougarou's curse, but I will do what I can to help you. You will need a very powerful gris-gris, one that I will create just for you." He replaced the bone bag beneath the counter and left the room.

Evangeline trembled where she stood. Despite the room's warmth, goose bumps prickled her arms.

From out in the shop came the sounds of canister lids clinking as they were removed and replaced.

Papa Urbain returned a moment later carrying a wide wooden bowl that contained an assortment of items. He set it on the altar, took out a small red flannel bag, and added the bowl's ingredients to it, reciting, "Root, bone, cayenne, snake shed, wasp nest, powdered blue glass, dried toad-stool, camphor, pigeon feather, and crawfish claw." Lastly, he held up the eleventh item, a pebble. "The most potent of all. Taken from the ground at the tomb of voodoo queen Marie Laveau."

He closed his hands around the small bag and murmured a prayer of blessing and protection, speaking so fervently, beads of sweat formed on his forehead. When he finished, he brought the bag to his mouth and gently blew on it, activating its power with his breath. He dressed it with drops of water from a small brown bottle labeled *Mississippi River*, then passed it through the incense smoke, and tied it shut with a leather cord.

"It's the best I can do." He handed it to her and narrowed his eyes. "Whatever advice your grandmother has given you, you would be wise to follow it."

Evangeline nodded numbly. He was right. Without the powers of a haunt huntress running through her, she was in no position to fight what needed to be fought on this night. "Yes, sir. I'll attach it to our client's weaken-binds, then . . ." She swallowed down the rock of a lump forming in her throat, willing her eyes not go teary. "Then I'll return to the swamp and hope for the best for her and her family."

He studied her for a moment with his piercing gaze. "Perhaps I can keep an eye on the family after you've gone." He cast a glance toward Beyza, the white crow, and she cawed in reply, dipping her head and rustling her feathers.

"Thank you, sir." Evangeline had not expected such a generous offer.

She reached into her satchel for money, but Papa Urbain waved her hand away. "There's no charge. Consider it a favor, from one professional to another."

"But I'm not a—"

"For your grandmother, then."

"Thank you." She'd taken only one step toward the

curtained doorway when his next words stopped her.

"The gris-gris is not complete."

She turned to him, puzzled.

"To strengthen the magic, you must use your own words of power."

"Words of power?" She had no idea what he meant. "What words?"

"That I don't know, but I can tell you where to find them." He pointed in the direction of the river. "Go to the St. Louis Cathedral. Stand on the church's front steps, and speak your request to the wind. The words will come to you."

Evangeline forced a smile to cover the distress rising inside her. There was no time for running around the city. It would be dark soon, and she had much work to do before she could leave the Midsomers and return home. The doorway woman's words of warning came back to her, sending her heart pounding. *It won't be safe when the sun sets.*

Not wanting to appear ungrateful for all his help, she nodded.

She tucked the gris-gris bag into her satchel and rushed out of the shop.

Evangeline hurried toward the river, past antique shops and souvenir stores. She passed clubs with strains of blues and zydeco music pouring out from their open doorways, past restaurants with the mouthwatering aroma of Louisiana's holy culinary trinity—onions, bell peppers, and celery—wafting out from theirs.

It didn't take long to reach the grand church, its triple steeples towering above the historic Cabildo and Presbytère buildings on either side of it. Jackson Square sprawled before it. Loud jazz music from a brass band on the corner bounced off the buildings and floated throughout the park. A young trombone player caught sight of her staring; he winked at her, and she blushed. Another blast of wind rushed by, swaying the colorful art pieces hanging for sale on the square's black wrought-iron fence, and bringing with it the distinct odor of the horse-drawn carriages lined up across the street. It blew tourists' hair and clothing, snatching hats from their heads and straws from their drinks, sending them gasping and laughing and chasing after the wayward items in the midst of the street party atmosphere.

For a moment, Evangeline was transported back to the fais-dodo parties she'd attended on the bayou. A pang of homesickness struck like the toll of a bell, and her heart echoed with a realization. These city folk and their guests weren't all that different from her own family and neighbors back home.

But there was work to be done. Sagging with fatigue,

she hauled herself up the church steps. She turned toward the Mississippi River across the way, the breeze tousling the tips of her hair. She had no idea what to say. She decided on the simplest option. Taking a deep breath, she whispered her request into the wind: "Send me my words of power. Please."

She waited.

Nothing happened.

She tapped her foot.

Nothing happened again.

She cracked the knuckles on her right hand.

She waited some more, feeling the minutes tick past as clearly as if a clock were lodged inside her head.

She glanced around the square, her gaze settling on the park's statue of General Jackson on his rearing horse. Atop his head perched a white crow, its blue-gray stare fixed on her. Evidently Papa Urbain believed she needed keeping an eye on too. She wasn't sure if she felt comforted or offended by his concern.

The bird kept its gaze on her for a moment longer, then sprang from the general's bronze head. It winged away over the square, soaring above the Lucky Dog hot-dog cart across the street. There amid the throng of tourists making their way up the sidewalk, towering a head taller than any of them, strode Randall Lowell, the silent, hulking giant who'd sat at the Midsomers' dining room table that morning. When Evangeline blinked, though, he was gone, already faded into the crowd, probably on his way to Café Du Monde for more beignets to bring to the Midsomers.

But if the weaken-binds didn't work on Mrs. Midsomer tonight, breakfast would be the least of the family's worries come tomorrow morning.

With a sigh of impatience, Evangeline closed her eyes, counted to ten, and opened them again. "Dang it, come on!" she muttered to the wind. "I don't have all day!"

A breeze whipped by, ruffling the gray feathers on a pigeon drinking from a puddle on the pavement. A dollar bill blew across the square. It skipped up the short steps toward her and came to a rest on the silver tips of her boots as the wind ceased.

Evangeline pursed her lips, gazing down at the unexpected arrival. She'd asked for words but had received money instead. Evidently she hadn't been clear enough with her request. She picked up the dollar anyway. One of its previous owners had doodled a pair of black eyeglasses onto President Washington.

Frowning, she turned the bill over and gasped.

17

One of the words on the dollar bill had been traced over with bright-red marker, one word from the line *In God We Trust.*

The word was *Trust.*

Evangeline thought on it for a moment.

As ominous as the red word seemed, she didn't know how it was supposed to be of help to her. She folded the dollar and tucked it into her satchel anyway.

Maybe she'd misunderstood the voodoo priest. Or maybe he'd been wrong.

Another gust blew, sending a fluttering lime-green scrap of paper flying onto the side of her face and plastering it there until she peeled it away.

She peered down at the paper, and her spirit sank even

lower. In her hand she held nothing more than a coupon for a local frozen yogurt shop. But when she ran her eyes over its print, there amid the black writing proclaiming the healthful benefits of probiotic organisms for your gut, two words stood out, highlighted in red: *your gut.*

Icy prickles ran down Evangeline's spine.

Trust your gut.

She knew those words well. Gran had spoken them to her all her life.

Fingers shaking, she tucked the coupon into her satchel. She didn't have to glance at the sinking sun to know she needed to hurry to the Midsomers' house.

She felt it in her gut.

Evangeline had no idea how long she'd been wandering through the streets of the Garden District. Or how to find her way to the Midsomer home.

She glanced around, desperate to spy any sign of familiarity. The sun was now touching the horizon, leaving darkness only a hair's breadth away. Panic clutched at her heart. But remembering Gran's oft-repeated words, she whispered them to herself: "Fear is a steel trap. It binds up your courage as well as your smarts." Gran was right, as she was about so many things.

She shook off her panic, turned, and retraced her steps,

rushing past mansions and manor homes built before the Civil War, the clacking of her boots echoing off the tall privacy fences surrounding their backyards. In the distance a siren wailed, a streetcar rattled along its tracks, and a steamboat's whistle blasted mournfully. The sinking sun finally set, disappearing like a stone beneath the water's surface.

Evangeline's feet came to a sudden stop. There it was again, the sensation of being watched, tickling the flesh along the back of her neck. She whirled around.

And again, no one was behind her. She glanced along the fence tops and into the tree branches, but saw no sign of Papa Urbain's white crow.

"Just nerves," she muttered, and started her feet moving again.

She hurried over the buckled brick sidewalks. And still the Midsomers' house was nowhere to be seen.

Darkness crept up all around her. Shaggy oak branches shrouded the gas lamp–style streetlights, which formed dim pools of light against the pavement. A few blocks over, a pack of dogs erupted into a round of fierce barking. "Fear is a steel trap," she reminded herself.

At last she turned onto a familiar side street. But just as her anxiety began to melt away, the clouds overhead pulled back, revealing a full moon gleaming down from the starry night sky.

A shrill, lone howl, something half-animal, half-human, erupted from the next street over. It hung in the humid air, lingering like a lonely echo.

Goose bumps sped down the backs of her arms. Whispering a curse word that would have resulted in a severe scolding from Gran, Evangeline slipped her mama's talisman from beneath her shirt collar. Even with the extra protection of the gris-gris bag inside her satchel, her palms were still sweaty with fear. She raced up the sidewalk, her heart pounding in time with her steps. Why hadn't she thought to pack some rye, mistletoe, and aconitum in her satchel?

The back of the Midsomer house rose into view. A few steps farther and the gurgling of their garden fountain brought music to her ears. At the sight of the tall wooden fence surrounding their backyard, the familiar clumps of large camellia shrubs and cluster of metal trash cans, the tightness in her chest loosened, and she almost cried out with relief. She reached for the gate latch, but her feet ground to a stop, as though suddenly bogged down in a thick pit of mud.

Something was watching her from very nearby, its stare nearly intense enough to gouge holes through the side of her head.

Evangeline stood motionless, not even breathing.

With a rustling of branches and leaves, a four-legged beast stepped from the camellia bushes. It stood not more than five feet away. The night was dark, and the creature was black, but she would recognize its glowing yellow eyes anywhere. The grim had followed them to New Orleans.

It gazed silently at her, twigs and bits of pine straw stuck to its matted fur, the smell of dirty dog wafting off it.

"Gran," Evangeline whispered, her heart falling to her feet. "No." She shook her head, and her voice rose. "No. You can't have her." Her voice rose higher, shriller, and she shouted and stomped her boot. "Go! Get away!"

When the creature didn't retreat, she snatched two metal trash can lids and clanged them together like cymbals, but the grim stood its ground. With a shout of fury, she flung the lids at it. They bounced off the dog's shaggy matted side, clanking and clattering to the sidewalk.

The grim bared its teeth and growled.

Evangeline took a step back.

Hot breath hit the base of her neck, and a foul odor rose in her nose, wild and savage and spoiled with the taint of old blood.

Thrusting out her mama's talisman, she spun around and came face-to-face with a second creature.

Red eyes glared down from the monster who loomed seven feet tall, his broad chest and narrow waist bristling

with wild brown fur. He snarled long and low, his dark lips quivering and exposing a mouthful of dagger teeth.

Evangeline's heart seized, and the strength drained from her limbs. "Rougarou," she whispered, the word slipping from her mouth like a dead, papery leaf.

At the sight of the talisman, the hulking beast staggered back on his two hairy, bowed legs. He raised his clawed paws, shielding his face from the power of the silver as though protecting himself from a blinding-white spotlight.

Evangeline whipped her knife from its sheath and held it out before her. The weapon trembled in her sweaty grip. Behind her, the grim gave another menacing growl.

With his burning red eyes fixed upon her, the rougarou dropped to a crouch. His snout wrinkled back, and he snarled again.

The hairs on Evangeline's arms stood on end. She tightened her grasp on the knife handle, knowing her weapon and talisman were no match against such raw, primordial power. Her eyes never leaving sight of the rougarou, she took a side step toward the gate, willing her legs not to crumple.

Flattening his pointed ears and flaring his black nostrils, the rougarou pressed his furred paws to the sidewalk, watching her, tensing his muscles, and readying to lunge.

Evangeline took another small step toward the gate, her

hand shaking so badly that the knife bobbed in her hand. There was no way she would make it to safety. She braced herself for the impact of claws and teeth. To the other side of her, the grim gave a deep, guttural bark. Snarling, its hackles bristling, it flew at the rougarou and bit down on the monster's left paw.

With a yelp, the rougarou bolted up. Sweeping his fiery gaze from Evangeline to the grim, he gave a lip-quivering snarl of his own. Then, cradling his injured paw to his chest, he hunched his hairy shoulders and loped away, disappearing into the night.

Evangeline didn't wait for the grim to round on her next. She swung the gate open and dashed through it. She flew up the back steps just as Julian opened the kitchen door and stuck his head out. "What's all the commotion? Did I hear dogs?"

She shoved him back, nearly knocking him from his feet as she rushed in. She slammed the door and locked it. Trembling, she scrabbled around inside her leather satchel for a piece of chalk.

"So, you have an abhorrence of dogs too?" Julian grimaced. "It's their noses I can't stand, so cold and slimy all the time." He shuddered. "Did you know that when dogs want to follow an odor, their noses create a thin layer of mucus allowing them to absorb scent chemicals and thus utilize their sense of smell more efficiently? They can then lick the scent chemicals from their noses, allowing the olfactory glands on the roofs of their mouths to taste those odors."

She'd just nearly been attacked by a rougarou *and* a grim, and this boy was afraid of wet noses?

"And their breath! It's always so rancid!" He closed his eyes at the horror.

Evangeline did her best to ignore the rising tidal wave of annoyance. She fumbled her knife back into its sheath. With her fingers shaking, she used her stick of chalk to sketch a series of protection symbols against the kitchen door.

"Hey!" Julian protested. "What are you doing? Stop that! You're defacing private property!"

"You don't understand." Evangeline was still trying to catch her breath. "These protection symbols will keep the beasts away."

From the other side of the door a set of claws raked against its surface.

Julian's eyes widened. A loud snuffling sounded at the crack underneath.

"It's the grim." Evangeline motioned toward the chalk marks, about to explain how they worked, when she stopped. Did she really want to keep the grim away? If she succeeded in repelling the creature, it might go searching for

Gran elsewhere. It might find her at the hospital only four blocks over. She rubbed her palm against the door, smudging the protection symbols away.

"A grim?" Julian raised his eyebrows in amusement.

Paying no attention to him, Evangeline nodded to herself. Yes. Let the stupid grim keep nosing around here. The longer she kept it away from Gran, the more time Gran had to recover, to rest up and grow strong.

"Grims, psychopomps, guides to the afterlife searching for lost souls . . . they don't really exist." Julian folded his arms across his chest, staring down his nose at her like a disappointed schoolteacher. "I suppose the next thing you'll tell me is that it's Cerberus himself, the three-headed hellhound who guards the entrance to the underworld."

But his words didn't needle her. Returning her mama's talisman to its proper place beneath her shirt collar, she bolted from the kitchen and raced up to her room. She ran back down, carrying Gran's steel-toed work boots and one of Gran's dresses.

Julian's mouth hung open as he watched her stuff the dress into the gap underneath the door, then push the boots snug against it.

Oh, but she was clever. Not only would the scent of Gran's belongings keep the grim here—and away from the hospital—but the grim's presence should prevent the rougarou's return. She smirked to herself. You didn't have to be an official haunt huntress to know that rougarous, and most other evil creatures of the dark, were afraid of grims.

"It's just a dog." Julian gave an exasperated sigh. "Honestly." He turned his attention to a large pot simmering on the stove. He lifted its lid and sniffed the contents.

An aroma of heavenly spices flooded the room, stopping Evangeline where she stood. "Is . . . is that jambalaya?" Her stomach snarled, grumpily reminding her she hadn't eaten anything since the beignets that morning.

Julian nodded. "Camille cooked dinner tonight."

Evangeline's legs went wobbly. She pulled a chair out from under the table and dropped into it. She rubbed her weary eyes. There was no way she could send Julian, Mr. Midsomer, and Camille out into the night, not with that rougarou prowling about. And Percy. He'd be at risk too if he drove up and encountered the creature waiting there. She sat for a moment, reevaluating her promise to Gran.

A whistle of wind rushed past the house, rattling the trees and shrubs outside. Evangeline rested her fingers against her satchel. Her words of power whispered back to her: *Trust your gut.*

She knew what she had to do.

"Sorry, Gran," she murmured, the cold hand of guilt tugging at her conscience. She would not be calling Percy to come get her. Not tonight. The people inside the Midsomer house had to be kept safe from the rougarou, and the grim had to be kept from the hospital, things she could not do while lounging around back home in the swamp. Gran's plan had to be adjusted. There was no getting around it.

But something else gnawed at her thoughts. The rougarou's behavior. It'd been abnormal. She'd never heard of one coming out so early in the evening. The beasts always possessed enough self-preservation instinct to wait until the very late hours before roaming the streets of town.

Had he come for Mrs. Midsomer? But that made no sense. The woman was already well on her way to becoming one of them. His actions just didn't add up, unless . . . unless the rougarou had come to attack another member of the Midsomer family.

Evangeline leaped up. "Julian, where's your daddy?"

18

Julian, still standing over the pot of jambalaya and holding its lid, shrugged.

"Mr. Midsomer's in his study," Camille said as she entered the kitchen. "He's reading a book, trying to relax." She set an empty tray on the counter and wiped her hands on her apron. "He's had a lot on his mind lately, poor man." She shook her head sadly.

Evangeline released a sigh of relief, about to collapse into the chair again, when Camille swept her hand toward the doorway. "You two go on upstairs. *Quietly, please.* I'll bring your dinner in a moment, and then I'll go sit with the missus for the night."

Julian returned the lid to the pot and left without argument. Evangeline started to tell Camille they could just eat there in the kitchen, but then she remembered Mr. Midsomer saying Julian preferred to take his dinners in his workroom.

Evangeline trudged after him. She would have to come up with a plan, as well as a backup plan. If she failed to keep Mrs. Midsomer weaken-bound when the change overcame her at midnight, everyone in the house would be in grave danger.

She thought on it as she went. One thing was for sure. Julian, Mr. Midsomer, and Camille would have to lock themselves in their rooms. She would draw chalk protections on their doors and nail up whatever pieces of rye and mistletoe she had. But it wouldn't be easy. They'd never agree to barricade themselves away. She had to try, though, and she'd start with Mr. Midsomer.

She hurried up the hallway and toward his study.

When she reached his door, she stopped and glanced at the loudly ticking grandfather clock in the foyer. There were still three hours left before she had to begin the process of weaken-binding Mrs. Midsomer, plenty of time to get everyone settled in and affix her protections outside their rooms.

Taking a deep, readying breath, she opened the creaking door. "Mr. Midsomer. I'm sorry to bother you, but . . ."

Mr. Midsomer sat slumped in his leather wingback chair, his head tipped to one side as he snored softly. A book lay facedown on his lap; the remains of his half-eaten bowl of jambalaya rested on his desk.

For a moment, Evangeline allowed herself to hope the remainder of the night would go this smoothly. She removed the old iron key, clicked the door shut, and locked it. "One down. Two to go." She tucked the key behind the grandfather clock for safekeeping and headed for the stairs.

But when she passed the dining room, she stopped. She fixed her eyes on the silver tea service atop the buffet, and an idea came to her.

Moving quickly, she piled the tea tray with as much silver as she could find in the room, pitchers, cups, bowls, and utensils clinking and clattering as she did so. Then she lugged her haul up to Julian's third-floor workroom and dropped it all in the center of the floor with a crash.

Julian looked up from his seat at the worktable, a wooden model of a trebuchet in one hand, a paintbrush in his other. He frowned at the heap of serving ware. "Now what?"

Evangeline didn't answer. She didn't have time for his picayune questioning right now. She dashed down to her room and took the rye, mistletoe, and jar of aconitum from Gran's valise. She shoved them into her satchel as Fader strolled in yowling up at her. She poured a mound of cat food into his empty dish and dashed back out.

Making sure each person in the house survived the night was going to take everything she was made of. With a gut-squeezing sadness, she remembered she wasn't made of much. All she could do was draw from the knowledge and skills Gran had taught her. She had no idea if it would be enough to keep the family safe. She would do what she could with what she had, and then hope for the best.

Back inside Julian's workroom, she pawed through the mound of silver, sorting out which items would best suit each person.

"For the love of God, what are you doing?" Julian had paused again, his paintbrush held in midair.

"Making sure you and Camille are well armed."

Pursing his lips, Julian shook his head, then returned to his painting project.

Evangeline was in the midst of divvying up the silver teaspoons when Fader sauntered into the room clutching a used Band-Aid in his mouth. He dropped it at Evangeline's booted feet, then sat and stared at her.

"What's this?" Evangeline furrowed her brow as she picked up the wilted peach-colored bandage. What use could she and Gran possibly have for such a thing? She dropped it into her satchel anyway. Maybe Fader was going senile.

Footsteps mounted the narrow staircase outside the room, and as a rich, spicy aroma floated up, Evangeline's mouth watered painfully. Camille entered carrying a tray topped with two Cokes and two steaming bowls of shrimp jambalaya. She stepped around the mountain of silver without so much as raising an eyebrow.

With a swish of his tail, Fader jumped onto the tall bookshelf and hunched down, eyeing the housekeeper and her food.

Camille cleared a spot on Julian's worktable, set down their dinner, and pulled an extra chair over for Evangeline. "Eat. You look like you're runnin' on empty." Then she left with her tray, again stepping around the pile of silver without a single question.

A wave of gratitude washed over Evangeline. Whether Camille believed in her methods or not, she'd never once scoffed at them. Unlike other people in the household. Evangeline shot a sullen glance at Julian.

The aroma of jambalaya drifted enticingly throughout the room. The evening was slipping away, but maybe she'd take a few quick bites, just enough to give her some nourishment and strength. Then she'd get Julian and Camille settled into their protected areas, and Mrs. Midsomer into her weaken-binds.

Evangeline didn't bother taking a seat. She speared a

plump Gulf shrimp with her fork, and as she raised it to her watering mouth, Fader leaped from the tall bookcase. He crashed onto the worktable and slid across it in a furry gray streak, knocking both bowls and both cans of Coke to the floor. He skidded to a stop at the edge of the table, gazing down at the rice and shrimp strewn below.

Evangeline couldn't speak. She couldn't even breathe or blink, her anger boiling to the point of eruption, more steam rising inside her than what had come off the hot bowls of jambalaya. Fader suffered no such paralysis. He turned and shot past her, snatching the shrimp from her fork as he went. Gripping it in his mouth, he leaped back to the top of the bookshelf.

Evangeline exploded. "Blast it! Fader, you worthless, no-good scat of a cat!" She stomped toward the bookcase, but he was too high to reach. He hunkered at the edge of the topmost shelf, the shrimp clutched in his mouth like the carcass of hunted prey. He gazed down at her and swished his tail.

"Dag blam it." Evangeline dragged her chair over. She climbed up, but it was too late. Fader chomped down on the shrimp and swallowed it.

She was too dog tired to fight, and too much work lay ahead of her. She gave the cat a withering glare and climbed off the chair. She joined Julian, kneeling alongside him, assisting as he scraped warm shrimp and rice back into a bowl. "I'm sorry. Gran's familiar . . ." She sighed. "Well, he's just rude."

"He's a dumb animal. He's not capable of consciously misbehaving."

"Oh, yes he is."

Julian's watch alarm beeped. He clicked it off.

"Dinnertime?" she asked.

He shook his head sadly. "Since dinner was late tonight, my entire evening schedule has been thrown off. Nine o'clock is normally when I go downstairs and watch *Dr. Who*. Now I'll have to move that to ten o'clock, and that will cut into my hygiene routine." He frowned.

Evangeline cleared her throat. Now was as good a time as any to break the news to him. "Um, you won't be able to go downstairs and watch your television tonight."

A look of raw panic swept over his face. "Is the TV broken?"

"No. Well, I don't know. But for safety reasons, you're going to have to lock yourself in this room until sunrise tomorrow."

He gave her a blank stare.

Evangeline thought it best not to explain the particulars of his mama's condition, how she would soon transform into a raging, bloodthirsty, hair-covered beast. That was information she could relay tomorrow, hopefully accompanied by the good news of his mama's recovery. "Don't worry, I'll place protections outside the door." She motioned to the mound of serving ware behind them. "If things get really bad, you can build a small barrier out of these silver pieces. Use a pair of tongs or a platter to defend yourself if you have to."

He opened his mouth, but before he could get a word out, a thump sounded from near the bookshelf. They both turned.

"Fader?" Evangeline gaped at the cat. He lay on the floor, eyes glassy and staring into nothingness. The tip of his tongue jutted out between his teeth.

An icy terror seized her by the throat. She rushed to Fader and dropped to her knees beside his motionless body. "Fader?" She tried to keep her voice steady, but it cracked anyway. "You better just be playing possum, you stupid cat." She nudged him with her fingertips, but he didn't respond. She shook his shoulder, and his head lolled side to side. His jaw went slack, and a thread of drool trickled out of the corner of his mouth.

"Fader!" A rock-hard lump rose in Evangeline's chest. Tears prickled her eyes. She shook him harder, but he remained as limp as a lizard's tail.

"He's dead," she whispered.

Evangeline's eyes blurred with tears. In the course of one evening, she'd lost so much: first her identity as a haunt huntress, and now Fader. And if Fader was dead, that meant—

Behind her, Julian cleared his throat. "If I might—"

"No!" She held her hand out to hush him. One rude and senseless remark from him, and she would lose her grip on the last shred of sanity she was clinging to. She would fly into a crazed rage, and all the silver, mistletoe, and rye in the world wouldn't protect him from the eye blackening she'd give him.

He wisely remained silent and kept his distance.

Evangeline hung her head. She was tired. She was hungry. She was alone, and she wanted to go home. She wanted her life to be the way it used to be.

"He's not dead."

Evangeline spun around.

Julian crouched beside the spilled jambalaya, holding a silver platter in front of him as though it could shield him from her wrath. "Fader's not dead, just sedated."

"What are you talking about?" She squinted at him, not sure she'd heard correctly.

"One of my phobias—my fear of waking from a drug-induced coma only to discover my face has been permanently painted with mime's makeup—led me to do a fair amount of research into anesthesia." He pointed toward the shrimp and rice scattered across the floor. "I believe the jambalaya has been drugged with a sedative."

"A sedative?" Evangeline's heart jumped with hope.

Julian cautiously lowered the silver platter. He scooted toward them and rested his head against the cat's side. He sat up with a nod. "He's fine. Have a listen."

She pressed her own ear to Fader's warm fur. A soft *lub-dub, lub-dub* rewarded her. She sprang up and threw her arms around Julian.

Julian's body went as rigid as a wrought-iron fence post. "Please let go of me. You're invading my personal space."

"Thank you." Evangeline released him and pulled away.

He shrugged. "He's just in a deep sleep. I'm surprised he's not snoring."

Just like your daddy, she thought. "Your daddy!" She shot to her feet. "He's sound asleep. Down in his study."

Julian's face paled as he stood. The door to the work-room slammed shut with a bang. On the other side, a key turned in the lock, and heavy footsteps pounded down the staircase.

They rushed to the door. The key was gone. Evangeline twisted the knob, but it wouldn't open.

"Camille!" Julian pounded his fist against the door. "Camille, you food-drugging villainess, let us out!"

"Shh!" Evangeline leaned close and listened. "Camille would never have done such a thing," she whispered. "Any one could have messed with that shrimp before she put them in the pot."

"Oh, really? Like who?"

Downstairs, people argued. Evangeline pointed toward the door. One of the arguers was Camille. The other two voices were male, and very angry.

Julian's eyes widened. "Burglars?"

Evangeline twisted the knob again. She stepped away, drew back her booted foot, then paused. Even if she could kick it open, what would they do? If they managed to make their way downstairs and past the intruders, then what? Run outside and hope the rougarou hadn't returned? She lowered her foot.

They were trapped good.

She turned to break the bad news to Julian, but he was no longer beside her. She spun around and spotted him across the room.

His head hung low, and he leaned against the tall bookshelf, appearing to be on the verge of a nervous breakdown.

"Whoa there. Take it easy." Evangeline held her hand out toward him. "It's gonna be okay."

With a grunt of effort, he shoved the shelf aside. It slid along the wall, revealing a dark opening behind it.

"Well, knock me down and steal my teeth," Evangeline murmured.

Julian grabbed the homemade crossbow off the table and slung it over his shoulder. "It's my secret passageway. No one other than Mother and Father knows about it." He cast a quick glance back at the opening, then met her with a serious stare. "You have to give me your word you won't reveal its existence to anyone else."

"Yeah. Sure." Evangeline was already poking her head into the darkness. "So this is how you appeared out of nowhere last night. Where does it go?"

"My parents had the inoperative elevator removed when they purchased and remodeled the house two years ago. This is the remaining shaft. My father helped me install a wall-mounted ladder inside that leads down to exit closets

on the second and first floors." He grabbed a plastic sand-wich bag of marbles off the table, stuffed it into the front pocket of his pants, and stepped through the opening.

"Wait! What do you think you're doing?"

He turned his gaze toward the superhero posters hang-ing on the wall, his posture straightening. "I'm going to defend my family." He gripped the ladder and placed a foot on one of its metal rungs.

"No you're not. You stay right here until we can figure out—"

Julian climbed down.

Evangeline huffed in exasperation. That boy was going to get himself killed as sure as she was standing there. She knelt beside the unconscious Fader, no doubt in her mind that the ornery old cat had intentionally saved them from eating the tampered-with food. She gave him a quick caress between two of his four soft, furry ears. "Thanks, Fader. This job will be over soon, one way or the other. And then we'll go home. We'll all be together again, just like we should be."

She stood, then scrambled into the musty-smelling passageway, working things out in her head as she whispered them down to Julian. "I locked your daddy inside his study. He'll be safe there. But your mama . . ."

Well, if she couldn't get to Mrs. Midsomer in time to attempt a weaken-binding, she would morph. And if these robbers should still be here, Mrs. Midsomer would kill them. It would be best for them if they took what they came for and got out right away . . . unless they were here *for* Mrs. Midsomer. Acting as some sort of vigilantes. A sick feeling seeped up inside her. If they somehow knew about her condition, they might have come to kill her, to prevent her from transforming at the stroke of twelve. Her stomach roiled like cream in a butter churn. "Julian, we have to hurry!"

They descended to the first floor, Julian drew a wall panel aside, and they stepped into the back of the closet, right behind a rod hanging with jackets and raincoats. They squeezed through the clothing, eased the door open, and peered out.

The men's voices floated over from Mrs. Midsomer's nearby bedroom.

"Ridiculous old bat of a woman. If we hadn't been ordered not to hurt anyone, I would have knocked her head in. Yelling at us not to mishandle her lady. As if we'd harm one hair on her beautiful head."

"Shut your mouth, or I'll bust your face," the other man said. "Calling her beautiful could be misconstrued as disrespectful behavior. And I, for one, am not prepared to die for your disrespect."

"Okay, okay," the other replied. "No need to get all riled up."

"In fact, don't say anything else at all. Let's just get her loaded into the truck and safely delivered."

"Truck?" Julian mouthed.

Evangeline strained to hear any sound of Camille's voice, but there was none. She didn't want to think about what that might mean.

Julian stepped out of the closet and into the hallway.

"Wait!" she whispered. She hurried after him, following

him into the kitchen and halting when he strode through the back door, which had been left standing open. She poked her head outside. "Hey! Julian!" Heart thundering, she glanced around the dark yard for any sign of the rougarou. That boy had no idea what he might be getting himself into.

A boxy delivery truck with the words *Perigee Dry Cleaners* printed on its side sat in the driveway. Evangeline was pretty sure the men inside the house hadn't come to deliver a bundle of clean clothes.

Julian leaped off the back porch.

"Dag blam it! Julian, wait! This is dangerous!" She hurried down after him, nervously scanning the moonlit yard for any sight of the rougarou. There was no sign of the grim either. She sniffed deeply, and the aroma of dirty dog met her nose. The grim was still there, hiding, and not off searching for Gran. That was one thing in her favor. And as long as it stayed put, its presence would hopefully keep the rougarou away.

Julian climbed through the truck's open back doors.

"Get out of there!" Evangeline frowned, waving for him to come down.

"You heard them." His eyes were as wide as a coyote-cornered rabbit's. "They want to put my mother in this truck and drive away with her. I intend to stop them." He paused, wiping the sweat from his forehead. His shoulders slumped, and his voice dropped to nearly a whisper. "I can't let them take her from me."

His words speared Evangeline's heart. She would have said the same about her own mama—if her mama had still been there. Her throat tightened; her eyes stung. This boy might not always show it, but he truly loved his mama. That was for sure.

She wiped her sniffly nose on her shirtsleeve. There was no way she could let him do this thing alone. He'd end up dead. Without haunt huntress powers running through her veins, she'd most likely end up dead too. But Gran's words had seeded themselves deep in her heart: *When you see others in need, you help them, even if it means a risk to yourself.*

Evangeline straightened her spine and drew back her shoulders. "Okay. I'll help you."

"I didn't ask for your help."

"But you're going to need it." She climbed into the truck and assessed her surroundings.

A narrow cot lined one wall. It'd been made up with a fancy lace-trimmed pillow and pale-blue velvet covers smelling faintly of lavender. Boxes were stacked at the front of the cargo hold. At the rear, between the wall and the back door, hung floor-to-ceiling racks displaying gray pants and turtlenecks inside clear, crinkly dry-cleaner bags.

If she was going to do this harebrained thing, she owed

it to Julian to be honest with him. "I have to tell you something." She took a deep breath then spat the words out before she could lose her nerve. "I'm not who you think I am. I'm not really a haunt huntress."

Julian pressed his lips into a tight line. "So you and your grandmother are frauds, trying to trick my father?"

"No!" She shook her head vehemently. "I thought I was a haunt huntress. . . ." She paused and looked down, forcing out the bitter truth. "I found out today that I'm not." She glanced up. "Gran's the real thing, though. I can assure you that."

"There's no such thing as supernatural beings, therefore you never could have been a haunt huntress in the first place." Julian shrugged. "Thus, you're still the same person to me."

Evangeline glared at him, not sure whether she should be exasperated or grateful he didn't care about her lack of haunt huntress status. Either way, this wasn't the time to argue. She cast a troubled glance at the house. While Mr. Midsomer would be safe locked away in his study, she had no idea what would become of Camille. She could only hope the men would obey their orders to not hurt anyone. At least whoever was behind this didn't seem to want to harm Mrs. Midsomer. But why in the world would someone want to kidnap her? Especially if they knew of her condition.

The silhouettes of two men appeared in the kitchen windows. They moved toward the back door, carrying a stretcher between them.

It was too late for an escape now. "They're coming!" Evangeline's nerves jittered something fierce. She'd rather face down a legion of Dixie demons than confront a pair of up-to-no-good humans.

"Let them come." Julian unslung the crossbow from his shoulder and thrust out his chest. "I don't know who these villains are, but I'm not letting them take my mother."

"What?" Evangeline's eyes widened with exasperation. "These men are professional . . . professional whatever-they-ares. You can't confront them. You're not one of those superheroes from your comic books and wall posters." She grabbed him by his ear.

"Ow!" He slapped at her hand, but she had a firm grip. She dragged him into a hiding space behind the crinkling bags of clothing and reslung the crossbow over his shoulder.

"Keep absolutely still!" She eyeballed the back of the truck, doing her best to slow the hammering of her heart, praying the men wouldn't discover them there.

"That hurt." Julian rubbed at his ear, scowling.

Evangeline had no sympathy to spare him. In a few hours, they'd all have a much bigger problem. And with the blessed ropes upstairs in Gran's valise, how in the world was she supposed to get Mrs. Midsomer weaken-bound now? The men, wearing the same gray outfits as the ones she and Julian now hid behind, climbed into the truck, balancing the unconscious Mrs. Midsomer on the stretcher. They quickly tucked her into the bed. "Let's move," one of them said as he settled the covers around her. "I want to get her delivered before she wakes up." He sat down next to Mrs. Midsomer.

"Yeah," the other man said as he jumped out. "And then she'll be somebody else's problem. Good thing it's only twenty minutes away." He slammed the back doors and climbed into the driver's seat. The engine growled to life, and the truck rolled out of the driveway.

Evangeline put her mind to it, but she was completely befuddled. For the life of her she couldn't make heads or tails of  what the men were up to. If Gran were here, she'd have had the situation figured out and under control by now. Gray misery curdled inside her. If she was the only protection Julian and his mama had, they were in deep trouble.

With Julian glaring at the man seated beside his sleeping mama, the truck pulled onto the road. Evangeline turned her gaze out the back window, and there in the darkness glowed the yellow eyes of the grim staring after them. The rumbling vehicle picked up speed, and the black dog faded into the night.

There was nothing she could do about the grim now, nothing but hope and pray the beast wouldn't realize her trickery and find its way to the hospital where Gran lay.

The truck bounced along the pothole-filled streets of New Orleans, passing old brick warehouses and rusty corrugated metal ones while the moon beamed down on them like a cold white spotlight. Evangeline fought hard not to fidget, her nerves so bad that butterflies weren't filling her stomach, they were dive-bombing it.

She pressed a hand to the leather satchel strapped across her chest. The contents inside were sparse compared to Gran's large valise, but she was grateful to have what few tools she'd stashed inside it, as well as any additional help the gris-gris bag might offer. Possessing no haunt huntress magic, she could only hope she'd find a way to make the items work. As Gran always said, *Determination leads to celebration.*

The truck slowed and turned into what sounded like a graveled parking lot. A garage door screeched open somewhere ahead of them, and they pulled into a huge corrugated metal warehouse. With a squealing of brakes, they came to a stop.

The garage door rolled shut with a thump, blocking out moonlight and streetlight, and leaving them in darkness.

The truck's back doors swung open. Evangeline held her breath, willing her runaway heart to slow to at least a gallop.

Without a word, the kidnappers carefully unloaded Mrs. Midsomer and carried her away.

Julian moved to go after them, but Evangeline placed a restraining hand on his arm. She listened as the men's footsteps echoed off the polished concrete floor and faded into the distance. A door opened in the darkness, then closed. All remained quiet.

She stepped out from the curtain of crinkly plastic bags, and with Julian right behind her, they hopped out of the truck.

Julian sniffed and wrinkled his nose. "What's that smell?"

"Lower your voice!" Evangeline hissed. She breathed in deeply. "It's fresh-cut lumber. And paint." She walked around to the front of the truck and glanced about, further assessing her surroundings.

They were parked inside a large warehouse. A dull orange light burning somewhere far ahead of them provided enough illumination to display a line of windows high above covered with horizontal blinds. Rows of posts held up the soaring ceiling crisscrossed with steel beams. Cloth bunting hung in swags from the beams; foil garlands spiraled around the posts. It was hard to tell through the dim light, but the place appeared to be done up in the purple, green, and gold colors of Mardi Gras.

"Where are we?" she whispered.

"I don't know." Julian gave her a sour look. "And if you had a cell phone, we could call for help."

Evangeline returned his sour look right back to him. "Well, why don't you have one?"

He crossed his arms defensively. "A number of studies have linked cell phone radio-frequency waves to the development of brain tumors."

"Oh, for goodness'—" She motioned for him to follow. "Come on. We can't stand around jawing all night." Midnight was drawing near. She'd soon have to break the news to him about his mama's condition. Not a task she was looking forward to.

She set off in the direction of the muted orange light, passing boxes and crates, mindful to soften the clacking of her boots against the concrete floor. They rounded a stack of plywood, and she stopped, the hairs rising on the back of her neck, her hand dropping to her knife.

In the distance, standing between them and the glowing light, a gathering of tall, hulking forms waited, motionless. They faced one another in two long lines, forming an alley-way running between them.

"What's wrong?" Julian whispered behind her.

"Nothing." Now wasn't the time to be getting a case of the heebie-jeebies. She forced her feet to keep moving.

They drew closer, the aromas of paint growing stronger, and the shadows dissolved around them. The looming forms turned out to be nothing more than a series of giant sculpted heads, each as huge as an outhouse, with eyes as round as dinner plates set inside scowling, jeering, laughing faces.

Their gaping expressions made Evangeline's skin go skittery. She pressed her fingers against her mama's talisman and moved into their midst, sweeping her gaze at their faces as she went. To her right, a simpering jester stared down at her, its head covered with a multicolored cap drooping with gold bells. Beside it, a bald-headed cyclops peered out with a single blue eye from beneath its creased forehead. She glanced to her left, and a scarlet-faced devil, complete with a set of horns and a pointy black beard, sneered back at her. "What is this place?" she whispered.

Julian pointed beyond the figures toward heaps of Styrofoam and a scattering of worktables covered with paint containers and miniature sculptures. "It appears to be a Mardi Gras float-building facility."

Standing so close to such large toothy mouths jangled Evangeline's nerves, making her fear that at any moment a giant hand might shoot out from the shadows, spear her with a giant fork, then sprinkle her with Tabasco sauce. "Let's keep moving," she whispered.

The orange light led them on like proverbial moths to the flame, toward the rear of the warehouse. They plunged through the sea of colossal heads and exited into a forest of parts, props, and pieces, reinforcing Evangeline's ever-growing impression that she and Julian had somehow shrunk to the size of insects. Flowers as wide as washtubs sat stacked on towering wooden shelves. Enormous vines and leaves stretched out across worktables. She and Julian wove their way through multitudes of huge rainbow-colored birds and fish scattered across the floor. No doubt this is what it must have felt like for Alice when she fell down the rabbit hole and into Wonderland.

Just when Evangeline thought things couldn't get any more peculiar, Julian stopped and motioned ahead. There in the darkness, row after row of long rectangular vehicles stretched into the shadowy depths of the warehouse. "We're inside a den."

"A what?" Prickles danced along the backs of her arms. Wolves lived in dens. And a wolf den was not a safe place to be if you weren't a wolf.

"A den is a building and storage facility for parade floats. Did you know that in the early years of Mardi Gras, floats were referred to as tableaux cars? They—"

"Come on." Evangeline cut him off before he could recite more history lessons. She waved for him to keep moving.

They drew closer, and the brightly colored creations came into focus, the long lines of floats creating a fanciful, otherworldly traffic jam. Some were single levels, some double-deckers, each one fronted with its own giant figure like that of a ship's masthead. Faint voices drifted toward them from somewhere ahead. She and Julian locked frightened eyes, then crept toward the sound, snaking their way through the horizontal lines of floats, tiptoeing beneath the watchful eyes of giant football players, caped superheroes, and bearded Spanish conquistadors.

The voices grew louder as they approached the last line of vehicles. Evangeline peered around the corner of a mermaid float, its sides covered with rolling blue waves and pale-pink seashells. She'd seen enough strange images inside this warehouse of wonders to last her a lifetime, but none of it compared to what now appeared before her.

"Good heavenly days," she muttered, unable to pull her eyes away from the grand plantation house sprawling right there before her, a stately southern beauty ornamented with towering white columns and red brick chimneys. Two sweeping staircases led up to a wide, spacious balcony. A line of moss-droopy oaks stretched along each side of it. A grassy green lawn lay before it.

The murmuring voices rose from a group of men in black suits gathered on the lawn. They stood facing the house and a narrow brick roadway that ran before it.

"What are they up to?" Evangeline mumbled.

At least the source of the orange light was no longer a mystery. Large firepots filled with dancing, crackling flames lit up the base of each white marble staircase. Another line of firepots stretched across the balcony decorated with swaths of white fabric draped from column to column.

Julian frowned and shook his head. "This is a clear violation of the city's fire safety code."

As Evangeline continued assessing her surroundings, she grew more confused with every detail she took in. Adding to the oddness in an already odd scenario, the bronze statue of a woman towered alongside the staircase to the right. Clothed in a toga and sandals, its shoulders squared and its chin held high, it must have stood at least ten feet tall. In one hand it balanced a bowl; its other hand clutched an upward-pointing wand, as though casting a spell upon the house's balcony.

"Why is there a house inside a warehouse?" Evangeline was seriously rethinking her recently improved opinion of city folk.

"It's not real," Julian replied.

"I know what I see." She scowled at him. "And I see a great big house right there."

"It's a façade, a re-creation of a southern manor home to produce the illusion of being outdoors on the front lawn at night. The oak trees are fake too, and so is the grass. I've heard of places like this. Businesses can rent this area to host private parties and events."

"A fake house." Evangeline raised an eyebrow at him. "With fake grass and fake trees. So people can pretend to be outdoors." She sighed with resignation. "Come on. Let's get closer and see if we can figure out what's going on here."

They tiptoed behind the line of floats, drawing nearer to the house and lawn, stopping far enough away to keep a safe distance between them and the men. They crawled beneath a float embellished with an immense jazz musician rising from the front of it.

Evangeline peered through the colored foil fringe bordering the bottom of the vehicle.

"Why are we hiding?" Julian whispered, kneeling and peering out alongside her. "I want to find my mother."

Evangeline frowned. "You're not very good at this stalking thing, are you?"

"No. Not really. With the development of the modern grocery store, we no longer possess the need to hunt for our meals."

She gave him a glare.

"It looks like they're gathered for some sort of formal event," Julian observed. "What does this have to do with my mother?"

Evangeline had no idea, but the midnight hour was ticking ever closer. She couldn't put it off any longer. It was time she told him about his mama's condition, before things started happening. And things were definitely going to be happening. She took a deep breath. "Julian. There's something very important I need to tell you. You're not going to like it, and I'm very sorry."

"Now what? I'm in no mood to hear more of your make-believe stories."

She cast a glare at him. His rudeness had just spared her the effort of trying to sugarcoat her next words. "Your mama was bitten by an alpha rougarou."

"A rouga-what?"

"A rougarou. A swamp werewolf."

He stared at her for a moment, then rolled his eyes and turned his attention back toward the artificial lawn.

"Did you hear what I said?" This boy was so exasperating. "Your mama was bitten on the night of the last full moon. That's why she's been so sick these past few weeks. Now it's the night of the following full moon. Come midnight, the cycle will be complete, and she'll make her first transformation into a vicious beast with an uncontrollable need to kill. There will be no way to reason with her. She won't even recognize you."

Julian remained silent, keeping his eyes on the gathering of men.

He was going to need protecting from his mama. Evangeline sorted through her satchel, but there wasn't much she could offer from her meager supplies. She took out the stalks of rye and the sprigs of mistletoe and tucked them into each of his back pockets.

"Hey!" He lunged away from her. "What are you doing? Invasion of personal space!" He reached into one of the pockets and pulled out the mistletoe.

Evangeline narrowed her eyes and pointed a threatening finger. "You keep that in place, or so help me . . ."

"Fine." He stuffed the sprig back into his pocket.

"When the change overcomes your mama at midnight, if she makes a human kill, she'll morph into a rougarou on the night of every full moon hereafter." Evangeline sat cross-legged and pulled out the red gris-gris bag meant as protection for Mrs. Midsomer. The chances of getting it to her now looked very slim. She handed it to Julian. "Keep this until we can attach it to your mama. Tuck it into your right front pocket."

Julian sighed loudly as he did so, but Evangeline wasn't deterred. She had things to say, and by golly, he was going to listen. "Once a person becomes a rougarou, the only way they can be cured is to destroy the alpha who infected them. However, if we can keep your mama from making her first human kill tonight, we can break the alpha's blood hold. It'll be tough for her; I won't lie to you. She'll still morph at midnight, but if I can get her properly weaken-bound, she'll survive and revert to her permanent human form come sunrise tomorrow."

"But wouldn't it just be easier to lock all these infected victims in a windowless bank vault until morning?"

Evangeline shook her head. "You don't understand. Even without sight or feel of the moonlight, the change would gradually overtake them anyway. The drive to draw blood and kill is maddening. If any of them were imprisoned, they would greatly injure themselves trying to escape, maybe even self-mutilate while in the throes of their frenzies. They'd most likely end up dying as a result of their wounds when they returned to their frailer human forms at daybreak. The weaken-binds are the most humane thing we can do for your mama."

Julian put his hands to his face and wearily rubbed his eyes, muttering something Evangeline didn't quite catch. But it didn't matter. She had no time to argue with this ridiculous boy. From her satchel she withdrew the bottle of holy water, and the small jar of aconitum tumbled onto her lap. She held up the bottle of liquid to Julian.

"What's that?"

"Holy water. If we can find rope or some other sort of binding material, I can use this to try and create a set of weaken-binds." Her shoulders slumped. "But since I'm not a haunt huntress, I don't know if my efforts will work."

Julian didn't appear to be listening. "What's this?" He picked up the small jar of purplish-black extract.

"Don't touch that!" She snatched it away. "That's deadly aconitum."

He wiped his fingers on his shirt.

"Also known as wolf's bane. Fatal to the human touch, and fatal to a rougarou. Extremely effective when smeared on the tip of an arrow and fired into a rougarou's heart.

Death is instantaneous." With a sigh, she cast a glance at the homemade crossbow hanging over his shoulder. "Too bad your toy weapon isn't the real thing."

Julian gave her a frown.

Evangeline continued, "Of course, shooting a rougarou through the heart with a silver bullet is also quite effective."

"Ah, another of your quaint superstitions, the old-world belief in the supernatural power of silver." He gave her the patient smile of an adult about to explain a complicated idea to a kindergartner. "Did you know people once believed the moon was made of silver? In early Roman times, women wore silver moon crescents on their shoes to ensure they gave birth to healthy babies. Here's another fun one. If you bake a silver coin inside a cake on January first, you'll have good luck throughout the year." He leaned in closer, fixed his eyes on her, and spoke his next words very slowly. "All of them the false beliefs of frightened, ignorant people." He sat back and steepled his fingers. "Silver simply doesn't have magical powers. And werewolves don't really exist."

Fury roiled to a boil inside Evangeline. She lifted her chin, her gaze boring into him. "An alpha killed my mama and my sister. I assure you, the rougarou is a real creature." Clenching her jaw, she slipped the holy water and aconitum back into her satchel.

"I'm sorry." Julian stared at the ground. "I'm very sorry

for the loss of your mother and your sister."

"Thank you." Her indignation settled to a simmer. Maybe there was hope for him yet.

"But it was probably some sort of wild animal that killed them. Perhaps a bear. Or a panther."

She ground her teeth till it hurt, fighting back the urge to holler in frustration. This boy was most definitely going to need protection, because if he kept on with his mindless jaw flapping, she was going to hurt him herself.

"Look, something's happening!" he pointed through the float's foil-fringed lining and across the way toward the lawn.

The men hushed their conversations and gathered at the edge of the grass. They stood facing the narrow brick road running between them and the house facade.

Off to their right and in the distance, more orange lights flared. Then slowly, the lights advanced toward them, glowing like alligator eyes in the night.

21

Four men emerged from the shadows of the warehouse. They marched silently up the roadway, carrying crackling torches that bathed the area with more flickering firelight.

Evangeline glanced from the torches to the firepots, mulling over the possibilities. Fire was one of earth's four elements. It represented rebirth. Was some sort of renewal ceremony about to take place? Or were they just going to set something on fire? Or maybe worse, *someone*?

"Flambeaux carriers?" Julian whispered.

Evangeline furrowed her brow. "I don't understand."

"Over a hundred years ago, it was the job of the flambeaux carriers to light the way of the night parades so spectators could better see the floats. It's a tradition that still exists among—"

"I know what they are! But what are they doing here?"

The fire carriers, dressed in gray pants and long-sleeved gray turtlenecks like those the kidnappers wore, drew up to the big house. Their faces remained stony as they bore their five-foot-tall iron torches before them. Oily black kerosene smoke streamed from the flames.

A sudden rumbling broke the silence, echoing off the towering walls of the warehouse. Evangeline tensed, and her hand dropped to the knife at her leg. She peered into the darkness the flambeaux carriers had emerged from, and a red tractor, driven by another man in gray, rolled slowly up the road pulling a Mardi Gras float hitched behind it. Ordinarily, such a sight would bring a feeling of happiness to the spectator, but the only thing it brought Evangeline was a heightened sense of anxiety.

The flambeaux carriers took positions along each side of the sweeping staircases. Then they turned and inserted the torches into holders in the ground and filed away to wait in the shadows beneath the large oaks.

Atop the purple, gold, and ivory-colored vehicle, a crowned king stood beneath ornate columns, scrolls, and fancy French-style gilding.

Evangeline curled her fingers around the hilt of her knife, waiting for what seemed like hours, as the rumbling tractor pulled the float to the front of the fake house and drew to a gentle stop.

The king, dressed in midnight-blue breeches and doublet, and knee-high black leather boots, turned with the formal mannerism of a ruler before his court. He faced the men gathered on the lawn. Evangeline's mouth dropped, and her brows rose. The pale complexion, the slightly large nose, the short brown ponytail . . .

"Laurent Ardeas!" Julian hissed.

If Evangeline had just been bowled over by a high-heeled hog in a house dress, she couldn't have been more stunned. Laurent Ardeas? The soft-spoken florist who'd quoted poetry that morning in the Midsomers' dining room?

His nostrils flaring, Julian glared at Laurent.

"Why's he dressed like that?" Evangeline whispered.

"It's the typical attire of a Mardi Gras king. Only the most prominent and influential members of society are chosen as monarchs." Julian's glower deepened. "He's obviously the leader of this charade and is undoubtedly suffering from delusions of grandeur."

A sharp-toothed shame gnawed at Evangeline's pride. Her observational skills were definitely lacking. Mr. Ardeas was what Gran would have called a wolf in sheep's clothing. Not that any self-respecting sheep would ever wear breeches and boots.

"Welcome, my family." King Laurent gave a slow wave of his heavy black scepter. "Welcome on this momentous occasion."

The men in suits bowed deeply toward him, murmuring as one, "Hail, Alpha!"

"The alpha." Evangeline's brain went buzzy, as though it were encased in a giant beehive instead of her head. "*Laurent Ardeas* is the alpha rougarou?" And if he was the alpha, there could be no doubt the men bowing before him were his pack.

She did a quick head count. *Thirteen.*

Not three or four, not even five or six, but thirteen. She squeezed her eyes shut, willing the world to stop spinning. A pack that large was unheard-of. If she hadn't already been seated on the floor, she would have collapsed onto it. She peeled her eyes open and cast another glance at the men dressed in suits, men who looked as harmless as any group of guests at a cocktail party. But these men were far from harmless. "We have to leave," she whispered.

Julian lowered the crossbow from his shoulder and slid the bag of marbles from his pocket.

Evangeline narrowed her eyes at him. "What do you think you're doing?"

He dropped a marble into the weapon's grooved track and pulled the bow back. "I'm going to exact revenge. *Not* from some mythological lupine threat, but from Laurent Ardeas."

"Are you out of your ever-loving mind?" Evangeline snatched the bag from him.

"Hey! Those are mine."

"Not anymore." She gave him a scowl. "You've officially lost your marbles—in more ways than one." She stuffed the bag into her satchel. "Little glass balls won't stop a rougarou. If you shoot one of them with one of these, the only thing you'll succeed at is making him mad and drawing his attention to you. And trust me, you *don't* want to do that."

Pouting, Julian reslung the crossbow over his shoulder and crouched lower, resuming glaring at Laurent as he slowly and ceremoniously descended from his kingly float.

"We have to get out of here," Evangeline whispered. "Now."

But Julian didn't budge. "I'm not leaving without my mother."

With a loud rumble, the tractor and its empty float pulled away, continuing down the roadway and disappearing into the depths of the darkened warehouse. Evangeline grabbed Julian by the ear and crawled backward, dragging him out from beneath the jazz musician float as he winced and batted at her hand.

"Goddess," Laurent's voice rang out, stopping them as

they climbed to their feet.

Evangeline tiptoed over and peeked around the rear of the float.

Across the way, Laurent stood before the tall statue towering at the base of the staircase. The flames from the firepots and flambeaux threw shadows over its bronze face, half shrouding its snarling expression. Cradling his black scepter in his arm, he bowed deeply before it. Then as he ascended the steps to the balcony, the men on the lawn turned. With the firelight bathing their faces, they too bowed toward the statue.

Gazing out alongside Evangeline, Julian gasped, his posture stiffening. "They're part of it too?" He directed a trembling finger at the thirteen men on the lawn.

A sludgy uneasiness oozed into the pit of Evangeline's stomach. "You know them?"

"They're Circe krewe members, the men who ride on the float with my father." Julian's shoulders slumped. "Men my father considered friends."

"Circe," Evangeline murmured. She glanced at the statue baring its teeth in a snarl, the cords straining in its neck. "Would that happen to be Circe?"

Julian peered toward the towering bronze woman he obviously hadn't paid attention to before. He nodded miserably. "That's her. Mythical Greek goddess, witch,

enchantress, sorceress—take your pick. It was believed she held an extensive knowledge of magical spells and possessed the power to transform men into swine or wolves."

"Wolves," Evangeline muttered. She pursed her lips, not surprised to discover such a connection. "Come on." She tugged his arm, trying to drag him toward the shelter of the numerous floats lined up behind them.

Julian fixed a serious gaze on her. "Please note my use of the descriptor *mythical*. That means she didn't really exist."

Before his words could cause even the slightest ruffle to Evangeline's feathers, his watch beeped. The eleven-o'clock reading-time reminder punctured the stillness of the warehouse with a rapid-fire round of chirping.

Julian fumbled to shut off the alarm, but it was too late.

All heads turned toward them, standing there exposed at the rear of the float and in plain view of Laurent and his men.

Evangeline's heart squeezed to a stop.

"Guests," Laurent called. "Join us." He beckoned them over, his regal demeanor never wavering at the discovery of two intruders, as though he'd been expecting them all along.

For a fraction of a second, Evangeline's mind evaluated her choices, weighing the options of fight against flight. Flight won.

"Run!"

She and Julian bolted away. They rounded the back of a Viking-themed float parked in the long line behind them and nearly plowed headlong into two men in gray. She spun Julian around. Another pair of the gray-clothed men stepped around the corner of a float fronted with a colossal figure of Cleopatra.

Two of the thugs lunged forward and grabbed Julian's arms. They hauled him away, struggling and squirming, and crying out like a cat getting dragged toward a tub full of water.

The other two clamped their grips onto Evangeline, but she shook them off. "I can walk on my own!"

She marched between the lines of floats and toward the fake house, her boots tapping hollowly against the floor, the men closely trailing her.

They crossed the green carpet of artificial grass, and the traitorous krewe members parted, allowing them to pass through their midst, their hungry gazes crawling across her and Julian's throats.

Despite her trembling, Evangeline forced her shoulders straight and lifted her chin. She wouldn't give these monsters the satisfaction of seeing her fear.

Their captors brought them to a stop between the two sweeping marble staircases. The flames of the flambeaux and firepots crackled in the silence around them.

Laurent peered down from the balcony, his impassive expression a far cry from the breezy friendliness he'd displayed that morning in the Midsomers' dining room. How had she not seen him for what he was? Even the most naive middling should have been able to sense such treachery.

"Let me go!" Julian struggled against the men restraining him. "I want to go home."

Laurent gave a disappointed shake of his head. "He who fears the wolf should not go into the forest."

Julian took a step back, his shoulders drooping.

A wave of misery swept over Evangeline. Gran had been right. She should've returned home to the swamp. She touched the outline of her mama's talisman hanging beneath her shirt, hoping to draw whatever comfort from it she could, and a sudden stillness settled over her, blanketing her with a calm, cool layer of confidence she'd never experienced before. Her pulse slowed. The colors and smells all around her came into sharper focus, as did the inflections in the tone of Laurent Ardeas's voice.

"I'm surprised to see you here, Julian." Laurent's face grew stony. "Cowards like you, so self-centered and oblivious to the world around them, seldom exhibit such reckless behavior."

Julian didn't reply. He kept his gaze glued to the ground.

Laurent turned and pointed at Evangeline with the heavy black scepter, its top ornamented with the shape of a snarling wolf's head. "I can't say I'm surprised to see you. Your kind have a great deal of difficulty staying out of business that's not their own. I sent Randall to get rid of you, and he tracked you to the Midsomers' house this evening." Laurent pursed his lips with dissatisfaction. "While he came close to doing away with you, obviously, he wasn't successful."

So someone *had* been following her when she'd left the hospital. A smidgen of pride swelled inside Evangeline, and she almost smiled. An alpha rougarou had believed her to be a threat to his pack. She glanced back at the men on the lawn, her eyes stopping on the tall, dark, and grumpy Randall Lowell, particularly at the bandage wrapped around his ham-sized left hand. He curled his lip, glowering at her from beneath his dark, bushy eyebrows.

She was glad the grim had bitten him. And if she was the one Randall had been after, that meant Mr. Midsomer and Camille would be safe from any more rougarou visits this night.

"However," Laurent said, reeling her attention back toward him, "I've since thought of a more appropriate use for you." Firelight danced in his dark-blue eyes. He pointed the wolf's head scepter at her again. "You're going to play a significant role in tonight's ceremony."

Evangeline's legs went weak, and her newfound swell of pride fell away.

22

"**S**eparate them," Laurent ordered.

With Julian giving a half-hearted struggle, his captors dragged him toward the left staircase. Evangeline's guards grabbed her arms and pulled her to the right.

"Let go of me!" She tugged away, but they dug their fingers in deeper and hauled her across the pavement toward the towering bronze figure with the cold, hard eyes.

"Dispose of her knife." Laurent swept his fingers toward Evangeline's feet. "And her boots. Their silver tips offend me."

Evangeline tried to squirm away. More men in gray rushed over. She bucked and thrashed and called them names Gran wouldn't have been happy to hear come from her mouth. But she was too outnumbered. They ripped her bowie knife from its sheath and wrenched off her gator-skin boots.

"Get rid of that handbag, too," Laurent added. "Goddess only knows what sort of contraband she carries inside it."

Strong hands pulled away her satchel. Then one of the men strode across the road and the lawn and flung her things away. They slid beneath a float spangled with stars and fronted with an immense bearded wizard clutching a crystal ball in one giant hand.

Evangeline had never felt so exposed, as defenseless as a rabbit trapped inside a wolf's den.

Somewhere in the dark depths of the warehouse, another tractor engine rumbled to life, leaving her no time for self-pity.

The machine slowly rolled out of the shadows and up the roadway toward the house, its mechanical purrs echoing off the walls as it pulled a new float behind it. Evangeline's stomach roiled, dreading whatever surprise would be revealed this time. She, along with every other set of eyes there, watched as the lavish vehicle inched closer and eased to a stop within the light of the flambeaux. With its cream-colored pillars and gilded trim work, this float also appeared to be worthy of royalty.

A woman stood atop it, and Evangeline's heart sank at the sight of her—though she couldn't say she was completely surprised. Puzzle pieces were snapping into place, forming a very worrisome picture.

From the base of the other staircase, Julian's confused voice rang out. "Mom?" He lunged toward her, but his captors held him back.

Mrs. Midsomer didn't appear to have heard him. She stood motionless up on her float. With a diamond tiara topping her midnight-black hair, white satin evening gloves to her elbows, and the rhinestones of her glittering white ball gown sparkling in the firelight, she looked like something straight from the pages of a fairy tale. Only one item marred her ethereal appearance: a black leather belt secured around her waist and connected to a T-shaped metal stand to keep her from toppling over.

Evangeline wanted to yell to her, tell her to leap down and run away. But then what? Come midnight there would be nowhere to hide, no escape from the devastating change that would overcome her.

From out of the shadows of the fake oaks, a woman in a gray skirt and gray turtleneck scurried forth like a gray rat. With head bowed, she climbed up to the float and unbuckled Mrs. Midsomer from the stand. She curtsied to her queen, then lifted her adoring face and smiled.

"Camille!" Evangeline's gut clenched as though she'd just been sucker punched.

"I told you!" Julian cried, his voice rising with hysteria. "I told you Camille was up to no good. I told you!"

When Mrs. Midsomer didn't move, Camille took her by the gloved hand and carefully led her down into the glow of the orange firelight.

Evangeline stood rigid at the base of the staircase, fuming at herself for not having detected this deception either.

The man pulled the empty float away, driving it slowly down the roadway, the drone of its engine fading into the depths of the warehouse as Camille arranged Mrs. Midsomer's hair and straightened the dress's long white velvet train.

From his place up on the balcony, Laurent cradled the black scepter in one arm and offered his other hand down to Mrs. Midsomer. "Come, my dear."

But she remained where she stood, staring vacantly ahead.

Camille took her by the elbow. "Right this way, my lady." She led her up the set of stairs, the velvet train trailing behind her. She guided Mrs. Midsomer to a position beside the king, the white swags of fabric and lines of firepots forming a regal setting behind them. Camille bowed and stepped away. Careful not to turn her back to the royal couple, she descended, keeping her eyes downcast.

"Camille, you snake in the grass," Evangeline whispered through gritted teeth. And when the housekeeper stepped from the staircase, Evangeline lunged from her captors and seized her by the left arm.

Camille yelped and tried to tug away, but Evangeline had already pushed up the long gray sleeve. She glared down at the fang and blood droplet tattooed on the house-keeper's inner wrist, the marks no longer hidden beneath the cover of a Band-Aid.

"A rougarou's human familiar," Evangeline growled.

No doubt all the men in gray were familiars too, the assistants to Laurent's pack members. Though in some of their cases, *prisoner* might have been the more accurate term. Familiars were often forced into servitude through threats to themselves or their loved ones.

"Take your vile hands off me, little witch," Camille hissed.

Evangeline narrowed her eyes. Then again, there were those familiars who willingly served for their own dark and twisted reasons.

While the guards struggled to pry Evangeline's hand away, she used her other to tug down the high neck of Camille's shirt. Instead of an ugly choker-style necklace, as she'd thought of it back at the Midsomers' house, a thick silver collar lay fastened around the housekeeper's throat.

"That's why you're all wearing turtlenecks!" Evangeline nearly spat the words with disgust. "To hide your pet collars, to conceal the silver's offensiveness from your masters—silver that's protecting you in case one of them goes moon-crazed, forgets who you are, and lunges for your throats."

Camille shoved her away, and the guards gripped her wrists, but Evangeline didn't fight back. She'd seen what she'd needed to see. She glared after Camille as she scurried off, straightening her shirt, then joining the other familiars waiting obediently beneath the trees.

Evangeline frowned at the realization of her own foolishness. Fader had tried to tell her about the deceit when he'd brought her the Band-Aid. He knew Camille was covering the tattoos. She'd even spotted a clue for herself when she'd peered into Camille's messy bedroom and seen the opened box of bandages on her dresser. And this morning when Laurent and Randall had stopped by to visit, Camille had made sure she removed all the offensive silver from the dining room, even going so far as to make sure Julian wouldn't be using his favorite silver spoon.

From his position at the bottom of the left staircase, Julian turned his pale face up to the balcony. "Mom! What's wrong with you?"

Evangeline knew full well what was wrong. Mrs. Midsomer was in the early trancelike stages of the metamorphosis. If Julian didn't like her behavior now, he wasn't going to be pleased at all come midnight.

Laurent placed a bouquet of white roses in the arms of the zombie-like Mrs. Midsomer, and a single white petal fluttered to the ground.

Evangeline's heart dropped with it. A fallen petal from a held rose was a sure sign of death. And if Papa Urbain was right, not one, but two people would die here tonight.

"The white rose!" Laurent proclaimed. "A beautiful symbol of purity, for our beautiful queen."

"She's not your queen!" Julian cried out.

"But why?" Evangeline shook her head, truly perplexed as she peered up at Laurent. "Why Mrs. Midsomer?"

Reverence filled Laurent's face as he gazed at his future queen. "Because she is descended from the pure bloodline of Jacques Roulet, one of France's earliest known werewolves. With ties to such royalty, she's more than worthy to be our queen."

"There's no such thing as werewolves!" Julian called, yet the slightest hint of doubt sounded in his voice.

Ignoring him, Laurent smiled shyly, then added, "The white rose is also known as the bridal rose."

Evangeline's lip curled. What a smooth liar he had been, bringing white roses throughout Mrs. Midsomer's illness, explaining how they were a symbol of good health, and all along planning to steal her away from her family.

Mrs. Midsomer remained motionless. Laurent took her hand and turned to address his audience below. "After years of planning and preparation, tonight we will finally be wed!"

Pack members on the lawn and familiars beneath the oaks applauded politely.

"She's already married!" Julian cast a glare up at Laurent.

"Not in the eyes of Circe, she's not," Laurent replied coolly. "And with the aid of one of our goddess's potions, come sunrise, she'll be born again, beginning a new life and new memories, with no recollection of those of her past. She will love *only* me." He caressed a lock of Mrs. Midsomer's dark hair. "I'll dote on her every wish. She'll have the best of everything. She'll be revered and worshipped and answer to the title of queen rather than the labels of *Mrs. Midsomer* or *Mom*."

Evangeline's heart wilted for Julian. Laurent Ardeas truly was a monster.

"That's not how love works!" Julian's scowl deepened. "You don't choose someone with the best qualifications and expect her to fall in love with you just because you want her to."

Laurent didn't reply. His eyes lit up as he gazed beyond his pack down on the lawn. "At last." He smiled the slow smile of a poker player who'd just been dealt the winning card. "Our other esteemed guest has arrived."

Evangeline followed his gaze. She tried to cry out, but the breath caught in her throat, and she could not draw air.

23

Clutching her firmly beneath the arms, two familiars pulled Gran across the lawn and over the roadway. Her head sagged. One bare foot and one cast-covered foot trailed behind her, scraping against the pavement. The men drew her to a stop below the balcony.

Someone had dressed her in a man's shabby bathrobe to cover her hospital gown. In her hands, she clutched the barely conscious Fader.

"Gran," Evangeline whispered feebly.

A crestfallen look washed over Julian's face. "Mrs. Holyfield?"

"Delivered as promised," a voice boomed from the darkness, "the old haunt huntress *and* her familiar." Out of the shadows stepped a portly gentleman with a bushy walrus mustache. "You can always depend on G. B. Woolsey."

"Mr. Woolsey." The name fell from Evangeline's lips in a hoarse whisper as he strode across the lawn. Mr. Midsomer's friend and fellow krewe member, the hospital president, the man who'd assured her Gran would receive the very best of care his institution had to offer.

And pack member number fourteen.

Mr. Woolsey stopped before the fierce bronze figure of Circe. "Goddess." He bowed deeply to the statue, then turned and bowed toward Laurent up on the balcony. "Alpha."

"Bring her to me." Laurent motioned to the men holding Gran.

As Mr. Woolsey joined the other pack members on the lawn, the pair of familiars dragged Gran up the stairs. Her cast-covered leg bumped along behind her.

Evangeline's stomach plummeted. She could hardly bear to look upon the sight.

Laurent stared at Gran's drooping head. When she didn't speak, he sighed. "If you can't run with the big dogs, old woman, you should stay under the porch."

Gran remained limp and motionless on the step below him, hanging between the two familiars like a broken marionette.

"Show me her face," Laurent commanded.

One of the familiars lifted Gran's chin.

Leaning forward, Laurent peered at her, then quickly drew back. The corners of his mouth turned down, and he narrowed his eyes. "Oh, old swamp witch, I do recognize you."

Fader raised his own heavy head and uttered a threatening growl.

"And your four-eared familiar." He pointed to the faded scar running down the side of Gran's face. "This is my father's mark."

The breath rushed from Evangeline's lungs, his words ricocheting inside her head. Laurent's father was the alpha who had attacked Gran. The one who had killed her mama and her sister.

Her thoughts tangled into a gray knot, leaving one fact hanging as loose and visible as a bright-red thread: Gran had killed that alpha. Gran had killed Laurent's father. And now she stood before Laurent, defenseless and vulnerable.

"Gran," she whispered, her eyes never leaving sight of the two of them.

When Gran still had not spoken, Laurent scowled. "Surely you haven't come to New Orleans to destroy my new family. What more do you want? I left your swamp."

"You ran away with your tail between your legs." Gran's voice sounded as clear and strong as ever.

Evangeline didn't know whether to feel proud or terrified. Laurent wouldn't take kindly to such sass.

He frowned down at Gran. "We had no quarrel with your council."

Gran spoke again, this time her tone as cold and deadly as a sharp silver blade. "Your alpha murdered my daughter."

Laurent took a tiny step back on the balcony, the faintest flicker of fear in his eyes. "Because you and your council planned to destroy our family! You left us no choice. We had to send a message, a warning." His brow furrowed, and he stabbed his finger at her. "But you didn't listen. You took your revenge against my father."

From his position snug in Gran's arms, Fader snapped his tail and hissed at Laurent.

Revulsion rumbled inside Evangeline. If she'd had a tail, she would have been snapping it too.

Laurent stared at Gran for a moment, clenching and unclenching his hands, attempting to regain his composure. When his breathing slowed, he spoke again. "No longer possessing our abilities, our family broke apart and scattered. I resettled in France, where it took me years to find an alpha werewolf who'd welcome me into his pack. And more years of loyal servitude before I received his blessing to set off and form my own family."

He gestured down toward the men on the lawn, as still

and poised as a pack of guard dogs awaiting the command to attack. "Now you come here to once again destroy my family?" His voice dropped and grew icy. "I won't let you do it, not this time. We're too numerous and too strong for you and your coven of backwoods witches. We will stay here in New Orleans and hunt as we please."

"You know I can't let you do that," Gran said.

Laurent shrugged. "As you wish." He half turned, as though to step away, then spun and smashed his heavy scepter against Gran's head, producing a loud *crack*ing sound.

"No!" Evangeline lunged toward the staircase, but her captors pulled her back.

Fader sprang away, and the familiars restraining Gran released their hold, letting her collapse to the step as they moved aside.

"Gran!" Evangeline cried.

At the base of the other staircase, Julian's head drooped, and his body went limp, leaving him hanging within the grips of his two guards.

Fader had already wobbled down the stairs. He made his way across the roadway and toward the line of parked floats.

Using the tip of his boot, Laurent nudged Gran's face-down body on the step beneath them. "Look, my dear." He looped his arm through Mrs. Midsomer's. "This is the wicked woman who tormented you with her country concoctions and threatened to bind you to your bed. You see what I've done for you?" He raised Mrs. Midsomer's hand and kissed it.

The corner of Mrs. Midsomer's lip pulled back in a silent snarl at his gesture.

The world wobbled and hummed around Evangeline, Papa Urbain's ominous words replaying inside her head: *Two people will die tonight.*

Laurent leaned down and grabbed a handful of Gran's gray hair. He lifted her head, watching as a trickle of red run from her scalp. Four drops fell to the step below. "There was no way to reason with you, old woman. You would never have stopped hunting us." He almost looked regretful. Then he let Gran's head drop, and he stood. But when he looked upon his pack members across the way, his eyes widened with alarm. "No! It's not time!"

Evangeline followed his gaze, feeling the blood drain from her face. Most of the men stood wearing stony expressions, their hands clasped before them, but others gazed hungrily at the red drops on the white staircase, their faces pinched and strained, their foreheads shiny with sweat. Two had dropped to their hands and knees, panting, their backs arching like cats coughing up hairballs. Mr. Woolsey lifted his arm and wiped his drool-covered chin on the sleeve of his suit jacket.

One of the two familiars holding Evangeline bolted away, casting bulging-eyed glances at the premorphing men on the lawn as he raced off in the opposite direction.

Evangeline yanked her mama's talisman from beneath her shirt and thrust it toward the men. The peculiar feeling came rushing back, bringing a keen calmness and clarity. Her mind and body refocused, sharply aware of everyone and everything around her. The sensation didn't startle her. It felt right somehow, like finding your way back to the place you belonged.

At the sight of the silver, Laurent gasped and cried out, "Take that thing from her!"

Camille was suddenly before Evangeline. The phony housekeeper slapped her hard across the face, sending Evangeline reeling. Camille ripped the necklace away, and with an angry huff, she stomped back to her place beneath the oak trees and flung the talisman into the darkness.

Wincing, Evangeline pressed her hand to the stinging line against her neck where the talisman's chain used to lie. She pulled her fingers away, and red dots stained their tips. It wasn't long before another man in gray hurried over and snatched her arm, securing it within his tight grip.

Laurent signaled toward the two familiars standing alongside Gran, then waved down at her motionless body.

"Remove her from our sight." He cast a nervous glance at the premorphing men. "Quickly."

"Should I find the cat and kill it, sir?" one of them asked.

He shook his head. "No need. It'll be dead soon enough. All haunt huntress familiars die within a few minutes of their mistresses. The two are inseparable in life, and so too in death."

The two men took Gran by her floppy arms, and while they hauled her down the staircase, another familiar rushed up and wiped the red drops from the steps.

Evangeline watched them drag Gran into the shadowy depths of the warehouse, anger rearing inside her and devouring her grief. They would pay for what they'd done, and if her actions were motivated by revenge, then so be it. It wasn't the haunt huntress way, but she wasn't a haunt huntress. She ground her teeth, her nostrils flaring. She would destroy Laurent's family. Maybe not tonight, maybe not next week, but she would do it, if it was the last thing she ever did.

With the sight and scent of blood no longer visible, the men regained the control they'd lost. They smoothed back their hair, straightened their jackets and ties, and wiped the perspiration from their brows.

"Now, without further ado or disturbance," Laurent announced, "it's time my queen and I were joined in matrimony." He took one of Mrs. Midsomer's hands in his. She stood stone still, staring blankly into the distance.

"Mom!" Julian yelled from the base of the stairs, his voice ragged, his face pale and sweaty. The two familiars holding him tightened their grips on his arms.

With a tattered antique book clasped in his hands, one of the men from the lawn mounted the steps. Slowly, formally, he made his way up to the balcony. He opened the cover, turned a few pages, and began reciting words before Laurent and Mrs. Midsomer.

"I object!" Julian shouted at them. He turned his desperate eyes toward his mother. "Mom! Mom, wake up! Snap out of this trance that villainous, swaggering fraud has hypnotized you into! You have to run away! Go get help, call the police, the army, the marines, the—" One of his captors clamped a hand over his mouth to silence him, but Julian's muffled protests still spilled through the man's fingers.

Up on the balcony, the ceremony continued, the officiating man droning on and on as he read from the old book. Evangeline blocked out his words as well as Julian's. She swept her eyes around her surroundings, taking in everything she could see, hear, feel, and smell. In the far reaches of her mind, a scattering of blurry ideas floated toward one another, blending and piecing themselves together. An unfamiliar patience filled her, and she knew a fully formed plan would reveal itself when the time was right. So she waited.

Nearly thirty minutes later, the officiating man slowly and formally descended the steps with the antique book tucked beneath his arm and a smile of a job well done settled across his face. The patter of polite applause drifted over from the pack members stationed on the lawn and from Camille and the other familiars standing beneath the oaks.

Julian's captor removed his hand from his mouth, and Julian wasted no time shouting up to Laurent, "That ceremony is nonlegal and nonbinding!"

But Laurent paid him no attention. Linking his arm with that of the vacant-eyed Mrs. Midsomer, he waved his black scepter in a kingly manner and addressed his pack below. "In celebration of this happy occasion, tonight we will hunt freely through the streets of New Orleans!"

The men on the lawn applauded louder, some of them whistling and calling out, the most animated they'd appeared all evening.

"Hunt for what?" Julian's face paled again as he tried to back away.

Panic clawed at Evangeline's heart, shredding her previous calm and confidence. The tourists, artists, and musicians in Jackson Square, all of them lambs in a meadow, oblivious to the monsters about to descend upon them.

What could one middling possibly do to stop them? Killing Laurent would certainly solve the problem. But to get anywhere near him, she'd have to fight her way through fourteen rougarous furiously defending their alpha. She'd be lucky to take down just one of them before the others ripped her limb from limb. Not even a true haunt huntress could evade such an attack.

"It's nearly the hour of the wolf!" Laurent announced. He spread his arms wide, his eyes gleaming. "Time for our queen to make her first kill."

"Are you crazy?" Julian gaped up at him. "My mother would never kill anyone! And she's *not* your queen."

Laurent motioned to Evangeline's guards. "Bring up the offering for our queen."

Evangeline dug in her heels, but her socks wouldn't gain purchase against the pavement. The men hauled her up the stairs as effortlessly as towing a pirogue across the surface of the bayou. They brought her to a stop on the balcony before Laurent and Mrs. Midsomer.

Laurent frowned at the hole in the toe of Evangeline's sock. Then he gave a sigh of disappointment. "A haunt huntress is still a worthy sacrifice, no matter her appearance."

"I'm not a haunt huntress. I'm just a middling." Evangeline never imagined those words would bring her such satisfaction. "My sister was the true haunt huntress." She glared into his eyes, her pulse erupting with anger and sorrow. "But your father killed her before she could live."

He shrugged. "Nonetheless, you're still descended from a haunt huntress, are you not? You underestimate your worth."

Mrs. Midsomer gasped, squeezing her eyes shut as the final stages of transformation began to take hold. Laurent patted the top of her hand reassuringly.

"Mom!" Julian shouted up at her, his voice filled with anguish.

"Fight it, Mrs. Midsomer!" Evangeline pleaded, though she knew it would do no good.

Laurent furrowed his brow and gave a small shake of his head. "Why do your kind persist in trying to stop such remarkable alterations?"

Curling her lip, Evangeline answered, "To keep filthy rougarous from killing innocent people."

"But innocent people die all the time." Laurent raised his palms. "More than 725,000 people a year are killed by the mosquito alone. What difference do our few hunts make in the grand scheme of things?"

How could he be so lacking in basic human compassion? "You don't need the flesh or blood of your victims in order to survive. You just maul them and kill them, and then leave them. Why do you do it?"

"For the same reason the housecat hunts the songbird. For the thrill of the hunt." His eyes grew shiny as he leaned closer. "Try to imagine the liberating power of the trans-formation, our bodies growing strong and immense, our senses keenly enhanced—results we could never hope to achieve in our mere human forms. No roller coaster, no game, no physical activity on earth can compare to the experience."

"You're insane!" Julian yelled. "Let us go!"

"Patience," Laurent called to him. "I'll release you in a moment."

Hope filled Julian's voice. "You will?"

"Of course. And I'll even make sure you're given a gen-erous head start before my family obeys the command of the moon." He fixed his gaze down at Julian. "And then the hunt will be on. Beginning with you."

A shrill chirping pierced the air as Julian's watch beeped the midnight hour, the indication that the time had come for lights-out.

The rose bouquet dropped from Mrs. Midsomer's arm, and Laurent kicked it out of the way. She cried out, grasp-ing her middle.

Evangeline's wide-eyed captors stepped to the side, pull-ing her along the balcony with them. She glanced down toward the men on the lawn, still in their human forms, but they would not remain that way for long. Even with the window blinds holding back any sight or sensation of the moon, the transformation would eventually overtake them now that the midnight hour had arrived.

Mrs. Midsomer fell to her hands and knees, her back arching beneath her sparkling white gown, her eyes squeezed shut, her face perspiring.

"There, there, my dear." Laurent knelt beside her and set his scepter down. He removed Mrs. Midsomer's gloves, train, and tiara and tossed them aside. He rested his fingers on her shoulder, repeating, "There, there."

The half woman, half rougarou whipped her head around and bit his hand.

He stumbled away with a gasp and a swear, the backs of his boots bumping into the scepter and sending it clattering down the staircase, where it rolled to a stop at the base of Circe's statue.

Mrs. Midsomer rounded on him, gnashing her teeth.

"Mom!" Julian yelled. He struggled against his captors.

Mrs. Midsomer's hands stiffened and fanned against the balcony floor, and black claws shot out from her fingertips.

Julian shook his head, his wide eyes fixed upward on the transforming woman. "No, no, no, no, no," he murmured. "How can I not have known about any of this?"

"I tried to tell you!" Evangeline yelled down at him,

feeling vindicated despite the severe mauling about to befall her.

Mrs. Midsomer jerked her head toward Evangeline, her pupils constricting, her blue eyes fading to pale green. She peeled her lips back and snarled a throaty growl.

Evangeline struggled to free her arms from the familiars' grips. "Let go of me!" she shouted, surprised when they actually did. She stared openmouthed as they fled down the stairs.

24

E vangeline tried to rush down after her fleeing captors, but her sock-covered feet slipped out from under her, and she fell, sprawling onto her hands and stomach.

Behind her, claws clicked against the ground as Mrs. Midsomer crawled closer, a growl rumbling deep in her chest.

Evangeline flipped around and scooted back on her elbows, her heart thundering.

Mrs. Midsomer's nostrils quivered. She lifted her head, breathing in the scent of the tiny blood beads dotting Evangeline's neck where her talisman's chain had been torn away.

"Mom, don't hurt her!" Julian yelled. "Evangeline's my friend!"

"Now, Mrs. Midsomer," Evangeline cooed. "You don't want to do this."

"But she's not Mrs. Midsomer at the moment," Laurent explained from a safe distance away. "She has no human consciousness. No sense of right or wrong to restrain her. In our rougarou forms we're simply not responsible for what we do, no more than any wild beast can be held accountable for its behavior."

Beneath her queenly gown, Mrs. Midsomer's spine arched again; the seams of the fabric strained against her growth of muscle and bone. Her mouth dropped and stretched, her jaw popping and cracking, fangs lengthening. With a snarl, the wolfish woman lowered her snouted face toward Evangeline, exposing her mouthful of stalactite-like teeth.

Evangeline squeezed her eyes shut, bracing for the storm of sharp-toothed fury, when a half-barking, half-crying howl erupted somewhere in the warehouse below.

She snapped her eyes open as it sounded again, the distinct baying of a hunting dog alerting its master it was in pursuit of their prey.

Mrs. Midsomer's lips slowly slid down over her teeth. She tilted her head, listening.

Out on the warehouse floor, beside a float fronted with a mammoth figure of Cerberus, the three-headed guard dog of Hades, the grim padded out. Its yellow eyes glowing like candles in the darkness, it stopped and fixed its somber stare on Evangeline.

The breath caught in Evangeline's throat. And in that moment, everything came together, revealing what she hadn't been able to see before.

She was the one death had been coming for all along, the one who would need guiding into the afterlife. Not Gran and Fader, but her. She was the one who'd been there every time the grim or some other portent of death had appeared over the last two days.

The shaggy black dog threw back its huge head and bayed again, long and melancholy, eliciting goose bumps along her arms.

Mrs. Midsomer crept away from Evangeline and paused, staring down at the grim.

"You won't interfere again!" Laurent's face clouded over as he glared at the dog, evidently recalling the beast's attack on Randall Lowell earlier that evening.

Another chance at escape would not come her way. Evangeline tore off her socks and scrambled down the staircase, casting anxious glances over her shoulder as she went.

"Sons of Circe!" Laurent shouted. He turned his gaze toward the men in suits pacing the lawn, obediently remaining in their place until ordered otherwise. He pointed a small remote control upward and clicked it. "Obey the command of the moon!"

With a humming and whirring, the blinds covering the windows high overhead slowly rose. "Attack the grim!" Laurent ordered. "Kill it!"

Cold white light flooded the warehouse, freezing Evangeline halfway down the steps. The glow from the full moon poured through the windowpanes, its draw so powerful that she struggled to pull her own human gaze away.

The men on the lawn turned their eyes upward, moonbeams bathing their faces. Some dropped to all fours, backs arching, muscles stiffening. Others stood moonstruck, staring at the windows, some of them whining, some of them raising their voices in cold, lonely wails.

At the base of the other staircase, Julian's familiars released their hold on him and fled. Other familiars scuttled after them.

As the moon's light spilled across the fake lawn and fake house, mouths dropped and jaws stretched. Ligaments and bones popped. Black claws sprang from stiffened fingers.

"How can this be real?" Julian murmured, shaking his head in denial. He ran his hands through his sweaty hair so that it jutted out at all angles.

"Julian, run!" Evangeline yelled, fear squeezing her heart, unable to pull her stare away from the transforming men. She was a deer, caught not in the headlights but in the moonlight.

The pack members' muscles and mass expanded as though being pumped with air, shoulders and chests forcing their way free from the confines of white shirts and black jackets. Pants shrank and seams split. Long, needle-sharp teeth, jumbled and crowded like those of a piranha, jutted from their black mouths. Brown tufts of fur sprang from their flesh.

The grim charged across the warehouse floor, past the morphing men on the lawn, over the roadway, and lurched to a stop at the base of the staircase. It set a paw on the bottom step and gazed up at Evangeline.

Evangeline glanced between the black dog below and the creature who was formerly Mrs. Midsomer waiting on the balcony above. She was trapped, but Julian wasn't. "Run, Julian!" she yelled again.

Snapping out of his bewilderment, Julian dashed away, racing toward the long, silent line of floats.

The last of the frightened familiars scattered like mice. They scurried through the warehouse, leaving their masters behind, looming nearly seven feet tall and sprouting fur, claws, and fangs. Some of them had torn away parts of their tattered clothing; others seemed oblivious to their ruined garments, leaving them to hang in scraps. Shoulders hunching, red eyes gleaming like embers, they loped across the lawn on their two bowed legs, growling in half-human snarls, their paws dangling at their sides.

Camille had not been one of the faithless escapees. From her position beneath the oaks, she kept her eager gaze fixed on her master and mistress, a dark smile tugging at the corners of her lips.

The first rougarou pounced onto the pavement, landing with the grace of a big cat but possessing all the raw power of a full-grown gorilla. He fixed his red eyes on the grim, and his dark lips peeled away from his jumble of saliva-slick teeth.

The grim whirled around from the staircase, its hackles sprouting like a dark picket fence along its spine.

The rest of the rougarous circled around the grim in a gnashing, slavering horde, growling and darting their toothy mouths at the creature.

The big dog reared onto its hind legs, stumbling back and raking its paws at them, whipping its head and snapping its teeth at those within reach, but it wasn't enough.

The pack descended in a fury, puncturing pink gouges across the grim's body. It yelped and cried out but didn't flee from the fight. Droplets of blood spattered onto the pavement. Clumps of its black fur flew. The beast would not survive long.

"Evangeline!" Julian crawled out from beneath a black-and-white-striped float fronted with a beret-wearing, white-faced mime. He rushed toward her, clutching her satchel and knife in one hand and her boots tucked beneath his other arm. Skirting around the grim and rougarou battle, casting worried glances their way but never hesitating, he stopped at the base of the staircase and tossed up her knife and her boots. Then he tossed up the satchel, turned on his heel, and raced back toward the floats.

Relief and gratitude swelled inside Evangeline, not just for the return of her things, but because Julian's delivery of them signified at least some small belief in their power and in her ability to use them. She yanked her boots on and threw the satchel's strap over her chest.

At that point, she should have run away. She and Julian were free, and with the exception of her mama's precious talisman, she'd even regained all her belongings. But she didn't want to leave. Nor could she bring herself to abandon the grim to face the rougarous all alone. The peculiar sense of calm and clarity had wrapped itself around her once again. She knew what she had to do.

She felt it in her gut.

She took the bottle of holy water from her satchel and poured a stream of the blessed liquid over her knife blade. Then, straightening her shoulders, she spat on the step below for added protection and fixed her eyes on the battling creatures.

With the grim's yelps ringing out, its cries of pain outnumbering its snarls of aggression, Evangeline raced the rest of the way down the stairs and past the ravaging rougarous, splashing the bottle's contents onto as many of them as she could.

The holy water hit their unholy backs and shoulders, searing through fur and down to their flesh like boiling-hot acid. A yelping, screeching turmoil erupted. Half the beasts tore away, whining and pawing at their wounds, fleeing like wildlife from a forest fire. They loped across the roadway and stopped on the far edge of the lawn, where they crouched and whimpered and licked at their burns.

Evangeline tossed away the empty bottle, smiling even though she knew she shouldn't. Without fear or the good sense that God gave a rock, she dove into the fray. She kicked shaggy brown haunches with the tips of her boots, the silver searing and sizzling rougarou flesh at every contact, the odor of burned hair filling her nostrils. Somehow knowing exactly where to aim, she struck with her holy water–doused blade, opening dark wounds along their necks and torsos. Her own arms and wrists were clawed in the process, but she ignored the pain. There was work to do. Pain could be felt later.

With ragged yowls, more of the rougarous peeled away from the fight. Pelts smoking, they scurried off to join their brothers in nursing their wounds.

Out of the corner of her eye, Evangeline spied Julian making his way up the staircase. His marble-shooting cross-bow was clutched in his hands, the stalk of rye clamped between his teeth, and the sprig of mistletoe tucked between his watchband and wrist.

Dang it! Why didn't that boy get himself to safety and stay put? Evangeline bolted for the staircase, but Camille stormed into her path and shoved her to the ground. Scowling like a cat caught in a rainstorm, the housekeeper rushed upward.

Evangeline scrambled to her feet as Camille ripped the crossbow from Julian's grip.

"Hey!" He whirled around, and she tossed it over the side of the staircase.

"How dare you! You wimpy, mewling boy!" Camille snatched away the mistletoe and rye and flung them into the firepots below, then clamped her hands around his thin arm, doing her best to sling him down the stairs too.

It was with no small amount of pride that Evangeline witnessed Julian fighting back, even if it wasn't the most graceful of defenses. He slapped and shoved at Camille, but he was desperately in need of a weapon. Evangeline turned to snatch up Laurent's scepter where it had rolled to the base of Circe's statue nearby, and she gasped, her eyes growing wide at the figure already leaning over to retrieve it.

"Gran!" Relief rushed through Evangeline. She wanted to shout and cry and wrap her arms around her, but there was no time. "Gran, get out of here." She waved her away. "Get yourself to safety."

"Nonsense." Gran seized the scepter. Using it as a cane, she clumped her way up the staircase faster than any woman her age with a broken leg and a busted head should have been capable of. She narrowed her eyes at Camille, muttering to herself. With tail swishing, Fader trotted along after her.

A few yards away, the grim cried out, still outnumbered by the attacking rougarous. Leaving Gran to deal with Camille, Evangeline tightened her grip on her bowie knife and dove back into the fight.

As more and more rougarous loped away, their flesh covered with cuts, bites, and scratches, Evangeline cast a glance toward the staircase, just as Gran swung the black scepter whooshing at Camille.

Camille stumbled back, tripping over Fader, who was strategically crouched behind her feet. She cried out, her arms pinwheeling, and she fell, tumbling and thumping against each marble step as she rolled her way down. She sprawled to a stop at the bottom of the staircase, moaning and sobbing. "It's broken!" she wailed, clutching her leg as it lay bent at an ugly angle.

Julian took another step up as his mama crept across the balcony toward Laurent, snarling and snapping and backing him against the wall. Laurent held his hands out toward her, murmuring, trying to cajole her into not attacking.

"Julian! Get down from there!" Evangeline yelled. Despite what he might hope or believe, his mama's mind was gone. The instincts of a rabid she-wolf had taken its place, and she would rip him limb from limb.

With only one rougarou remaining in the fight, Evangeline leaped away from the grim. The two beasts crashed to the pavement, rolling and snapping and snarling, dark fur flying. She hurried up the staircase.

Drawing ever closer to the balcony, Julian moved to take another step up, but Gran tugged him back.

"Mom, it's me, Julian!" he called.

Mrs. Midsomer stopped in midcrawl. She turned away from Laurent and toward Julian, tilting her head like a pet recognizing the sound of its name.

Despite knowing better, a small hope flickered inside Evangeline, and she paused. Was it possible some part of the woman still knew her son? Was Mrs. Midsomer somehow able to distinguish his voice through the fog in her mind, the way she had heard him reading to her all those times when she'd been asleep?

"No, no, my dear." Laurent cupped his hand to Mrs. Midsomer's pale face and turned it toward his. "Don't listen to the boy."

Mrs. Midsomer bared her teeth at Laurent and whipped her head back toward Julian on the staircase.

Shaking Gran's hand away, Julian took another step up. Mrs. Midsomer watched him with her blazing green gaze. "Mom?" he said softly.

"Enough!" Laurent shouted, his face darkening. He kicked off his black boots and pointed a finger down at Julian. "You are a distraction who must be removed. Then my queen will be free to fully transform. And you, old woman." He rounded on Gran. "This time I'll make sure your heart stops, and I'll do it with my own claws."

25

Laurent thrust his head back and gazed toward the high windows, up at the white orb shining down like a hole cut through the night sky. His eyes grew round, the light reflecting brightly inside them, and his pupils constricted, as though to look the moon's power behind them. His mouth stretched wide, popping and cracking as his teeth lengthened and sharpened like skewers. Claws burst from his toes and fingertips. Silvery-gray fur sprouted from his flesh.

Midway up the staircase Evangeline paused. She tightened her grip on her knife. She tried to yell, but her voice came out like a frog's croak instead: "Gran. Julian."

Camille dragged herself across the floor, casting glances up at her morphing master as his chest broadened. He tore off the doublet and flung it away. His leg bones stretched

and bowed, his dark blue breeches shrinking above his hairy knees.

Evangeline remained as paralyzed as Gran and Julian appeared to be. The Laurent rougarou stood a foot taller than any of his pack members. There could be no doubt he was the alpha. Not only was he able to maintain control over his transformation and morph at will, he was also physically grander in every way. His silver-gray fur lay smooth and sleek, not scruffy like that of the other rougarous, and his eyes blazed a piercing blue instead of red.

Alpha Laurent roared, spittle flying from his ridge of razor teeth. With shoulders hunched, he clomped from the back of the balcony toward the steps on his two furry, bent legs.

Near the top of the staircase, Gran positioned herself in front of Julian, swinging the scepter at the oncoming monster. "Run, Julian," she ordered. "I'll hold this beast off."

Julian shook his head. "I'm not leaving my mother!"

Icy sweat broke out against the back of Evangeline's neck. There was no way this standoff would end in their favor. The scepter wasn't much of a weapon, not against an alpha rougarou. And with her broken leg, Gran was no match for him either. He would kill the both of them, and he would do so with two easy swipes of his killer claws.

Snarling and snapping, Mrs. Midsomer pounced onto

Laurent's back, driving her claws into his shoulders and sinking her fangs into his neck.

"No, Mom!" Julian yelled.

With a thunderous growl, Laurent swung his paw around, slamming it into the side of Mrs. Midsomer's head and knocking her away.

She fell in a tumble, then scrambled onto her hands and knees, the muscles bunching on her enlarged forearms. She darted forward again, this time sinking her sharp teeth into his leg.

If Evangeline had doubted before, she no longer did. There was no question part of Mrs. Midsomer was still aware, the part driven by a love so strong, she'd sacrifice herself to protect her son.

Laurent tore the woman away and flung her against the wall of the house. She impacted with a yelp and crashed down onto one of the firepots, sending hot coals and flames scattering across the balcony.

Mrs. Midsomer lay motionless in an unconscious heap, half woman, half wolf in a beaded satin gown.

Flames raced up the wooden columns and jumped to the white fabric draped between them. Laurent raised his snout and wailed mournfully.

"Mom!" Julian cried. Gran put a restraining arm around his shoulder.

Time was up. Evangeline saw it as clearly as a clock hand ticking onto the number twelve. Laurent would round on Julian and Gran. His animal fury would know no bounds. She pressed her hand to the place where her mama's talisman used to rest, and her newfound focus and courage grew even stronger.

She swept her eyes over her surroundings, from the balcony's burning drapes down to the tips of Circe's bronze sandals. She knew what she needed to do. Her next course of action lay before her so distinctly, she could almost see it shimmering like a movie projection.

Quantity, angles, and velocity were concepts she'd never thought much about, and she didn't really contemplate them now. They were just there. Everything connecting. Everything clear.

Placing all her faith in her senses and instincts, she took the jar of aconitum from her satchel.

There would be no going back. But this was the only way. The alpha's blood hold over his pack had to be broken. Laurent had to be destroyed.

She dipped her knife tip into the dark, deadly extract and returned the jar to her satchel.

Hot flames from the drapery had spread, now racing their way up the wall of the fake house and jumping onto its roof. Thick smoke rolled against the beams of the warehouse ceiling.

Alpha Laurent reeled around on his hairy clawed feet and tromped toward Julian and Gran on the stairs. He bellowed a roar, his electric-blue eyes flashing with fury.

Despite his previous protestation, Julian took a step down, and then another. He and the scepter-swinging Gran slowly descended the staircase as Evangeline raced up and past them.

"Evangeline, stay back!" Gran commanded, but Evangeline didn't listen.

She leaped onto the balcony and in front of Laurent. Bracing her booted feet, she drew back her knife arm. There was no need for guesswork. She sensed the location of the alpha's heart, its pulsing and poundings somehow visible to her eyes and her ears.

Laurent swung a huge paw, his claws swooshing through air and brushing the tips of her hair as she ducked. She sprang up, reared her arm back again, and drove her knife toward his chest.

But the alpha rougarou's reflexes were unhumanly fast, and the blade impaled in his forearm instead. It was enough distraction to allow Evangeline to dash to the right.

Bellowing, he yanked the knife free. He grasped it in both meaty paws and snapped the hilt from the blade, then flung the pieces to the pavement below.

"Come on . . . ," Evangeline urged him as she backed away. She slipped her hand into her satchel, sidling closer to the balcony railing until she bumped into it.

Snarling, the monster who had once been Laurent Ardeas stalked toward her.

She withdrew the aconitum, opening the jar as she turned away from him. Not thinking, letting her hands do the work on their own, she shook the purplish-black contents over the edge of the balcony, hoping her plan would succeed.

Thick claws clicked against the floor behind her. The alpha's hot breath hit the base of her neck.

"Hey!" Julian yelled from the top of the staircase.

Evangeline spun toward him as he flung a handful of marbles at the rougarou.

It was the last break of luck she needed. The marbles bounced off the beast and clattered to the pavement like glass raindrops.

She fixed her eyes on Julian's frightened ones. "Thank you," she whispered. He was afraid, but Julian Midsomer was not a coward, despite what Laurent or anyone else might think.

Laurent rounded on him with an earsplitting roar. If Julian's plan had been to make the beast mad and draw his attention toward him, he'd succeeded.

The rougarou lunged for Julian, one huge foot coming down on the marbles and skating out from under him. He clutched at the air as he righted his balance. Julian turned and raced down the staircase, probably hoping Evangeline would be right behind him, but she was not.

She darted from the railing and around to face Laurent, standing between him and the retreating Julian. "Hey, Big and Ugly!" She chucked the empty aconitum jar at him, and it bounced off his black nose, drawing his focus from Julian.

With her eyes locked on the alpha, she stepped around him again, this time backing toward the burning house instead of the balcony. She pressed her shoulders against the wall. Above her the flaming fabric crackled and smoked, the heat warming the top of her head.

Laurent turned, and, fixing his glowing blue glare on her, he took a step toward her, peeling back his lips and baring his fangs with a snarl.

Evangeline didn't dwell on what she had to do next. She shot toward him without any thought, rushing across the short distance, leaping and throwing her full body weight into his chest. She wrapped her arms and legs around him, clutching his thick fur with as much strength as her hands would provide.

Laurent stumbled backward, his big clawed feet coming

down unsteadily on more marbles, the misstep driving him into the balcony railing and sending him toppling over the side.

Girl and monster hurtled toward the pavement below.

Laurent's rougarou body crashed onto Circe's statue. The tip of its upward-pointing wand punched through his silver-gray back. It ran through his heart, exiting his chest and piercing Evangeline's shoulder.

The puncture burned and seared, and Evangeline cried out as the statue toppled beneath their weight. They crashed to the ground, the impact throwing her free from the wand.

The rougarou and the statue rolled to a stop, Laurent's grand alpha body already morphing into his small, pallid human form. A rivulet of blood trickled from the corner of his mouth.

Evangeline's mind was muddled and foggy, but one thought rose through the mist: the voodoo priest had been right. There had been bloodshed this night, and there had been death. Laurent's was the first.

She pressed a hand to her bleeding shoulder. The stab wound wasn't life-threatening.

She climbed to her feet, and everything went wavy.

No, the wound wasn't lethal. But the aconitum she'd dumped over the balcony and onto the tip of Circe's wand was.

Evangeline's legs collapsed, and she dropped to the pavement.

As the last of her life slipped away, she watched Laurent's pack return to their human forms. With their clothing hanging in tatters, they ran, disappearing into the warehouse. Camille, her face squeezed tight with agony, and dragging her broken leg behind her, crawled into the darkness after them. Not far away, the grim lay on its side, blood trickling from its many wounds, the glow in its yellow eyes fading.

Gran hobbled over and dropped down beside Evangeline.

"Gran, I think I might have some haunt huntress powers after all," Evangeline whispered.

"I'm sure you do." Gran grasped Evangeline's scratched and punctured wrist in her warm hand, feeling for her pulse.

"Imagine what my sister and I could have accomplished together if she'd been here to help." Evangeline managed a pained smile. "We would have been unstoppable."

Fader scampered across the pavement, a necklace chain dangling from his mouth. He dropped it into the palm of Evangeline's upturned hand.

She closed her fingers around her mama's silver talisman. "Thanks, Fader." She shut her eyes. "I think Mama would have been proud of me, don't you, Gran?"

"I do indeed," Gran murmured. "You've proven yourself

to be a haunt huntress any mama, *and grandmama*, would be proud of."

Evangeline smiled. "I am a haunt huntress."

Her heart slowed, the beats coming fewer and farther between.

The world and reality faded away, and the last words she heard Gran speak were "Go get her!"

Evangeline's heart beat its last, and she died.

26

It was dark. And silent. Evangeline couldn't feel her body, but she was still herself. A pinprick of light appeared in the blackness surrounding her, so she moved toward it. The light in the dark was welcoming.

A presence emerged behind her, and she turned. There in the dimness stood the grim, with its yellow eyes fixed on her.

"Are you here to lead me to the other side? There's no need."

When the grim didn't leave, she sighed. "Well, lead on then."

Another pinprick of light appeared behind the beast. Another appeared to her left, one to her right, two above, three below. More of them winked into existence all around her, dotting the blackness like orange stars in the sky. There were so many to choose from. Maybe she did need the grim to lead her to the right one after all.

The big dog turned and walked away. She followed it toward one of the pinpricks, and as they drew closer, the light expanded, swelling into an orange glow.

The rougarou wounds on her arms and wrists stung something fierce. Her pierced shoulder burned and throbbed. And the afterworld smelled smoky. This was eternity? Where was the peace and all-encompassing beauty? No wonder so many spirits became restless.

A tongue licked her face.

She squinted her eyes open.

The orange light flared too bright, too intense. She wrinkled her nose at the burning smell. The grim licked her face, and her eyes flew the rest of the way open.

Orange embers and black ashes floated all around her. Acrid smoke filled her nose.

Gran peered down at her.

Gran was dead too?

And there was Julian. And his mama.

Her sacrifice had been for nothing? A rush of anger surged through her, and she cursed out loud.

Gran frowned. "Language, Evangeline."

Mrs. Midsomer smiled. Her hair was mussed. Her

beautiful ball gown was filthy. At least her teeth were no longer fang shaped and her eyes no longer lit green. "I'll be back as soon as I can," she murmured, and hurried away.

"I'm sorry I couldn't save you all," Evangeline rasped, feeling as weak as dishwater.

A look of confusion crossed Julian's face, and then he laughed out loud.

Even in death, he wouldn't take her seriously. Annoyance buzzed inside her. It was going to be a long, miserable afterlife.

"We're not dead. And you're not either." The smile slipped from his face. "At least, you're not dead anymore."

She narrowed her eyes at him. He was making no sense at all.

"You stopped breathing. And your heart stopped." He hesitated, running a hand through his already disheveled hair. "You actually died. But then the grim brought you back." He motioned toward the black dog looming nearby.

"Back?"

Julian nodded, his expression still sober. "The grim crawled toward you and sort of collapsed next to you. Then your gran told it to go fetch your soul. It took it a while to climb to its feet, because of all its injuries, but when it finally did, it just stood there, staring off into space. Then the next thing we knew, you were breathing again."

Evangeline still couldn't make heads or tails out of what he was saying. Grims only took you one way, and that was *to* the afterlife, not away from it.

She turned her gaze toward Gran. "Gran?" she asked, her voice scratchy and hoarse. "What's this boy going on about?"

"Don't you know?" Gran looked completely worn-out and beaten. She rested her hand against Evangeline's cheek and gave her a tired smile. "He's been searching for you all this time."

"Who, Gran? Who's been searching for me?"

"Your familiar."

"My familiar?" Her heart lurched, bringing with it a wave of dizziness.

The smell of dirty dog filled her nostrils. With a whine, the grim plopped down and rested his head on her booted feet.

Evangeline stared down at the creature. She wrinkled her forehead. "Are you trying to tell me . . . this grim . . . is my familiar? How can that be?"

"Well, it hasn't happened often," Gran said. "But it's not unheard of with unique birth circumstances like yours." She paused, her eyebrows gathering. "Though I'm not sure there's ever been a birth circumstance quite like yours."

Evangeline squinted at the black dog. "The grim. The

grim is my familiar." Her thoughts felt as thick as mud. Perhaps her mind was experiencing death-lag.

"It's a haunt huntress's developing powers that call her familiar to her," Gran continued. "Your call was weak, half powered because it appears you inherited half the power. He must have been searching for you for quite a while."

"I . . . I kept seeing him, but I thought he was coming for you because"—Evangeline lowered her voice—"because you're getting old."

"Nonsense." Gran waved the notion away. "I'm not going anywhere anytime soon. I'm as strong as a mule."

"Gran." Tears welled in Evangeline's eyes. "I thought Laurent had killed you."

Gran drew the scepter near and pointed to a fracture near the top of it. "It was the wood that cracked, not my skull. I told you I had a hard head."

A tornado of emotions overtook Evangeline: shame for having tried to run the grim off all those times, shock, awe, pride, excitement, and, oddly enough, a bit of shyness. She fixed her gaze on the big dog again. "So, you're my familiar?"

The grim moved closer and rested his head against her noninjured shoulder.

Evangeline swallowed hard, surprised at the lump forming in her throat and the tears threatening to well up again.

"Now all I have to do is prove I have heart," she whispered.

"The true proof of heart," Gran said, "is helping others in need, even when doing so will come at a steep personal cost. I'm sure the council will agree you more than demonstrated that tonight."

Gran's words filled Evangeline with a gratification she'd never known. Struggling, she sat up, wincing at the various sites of pain lighting up all over her body. She turned to the grim, and her heart sank. His snout and coat were covered with gashes and matted with blood. "Oh, Gran! He's hurt!"

"We'll get him fixed up." Gran took her by the hand and helped her to her feet.

Another jolt of pain surged through her shoulder. "Where are we going?"

"We have to get out of here." Julian pointed toward the flames dancing across the house's roof. Some of the floats had already caught fire. "The whole place will go up soon."

Mrs. Midsomer was back. She jingled a ring of keys. "We're in luck. They were still in Laurent's convertible."

Evangeline cast a glance at his lifeless form. "What about Laurent?" But if someone gave her an answer, she didn't hear it. The world went spinny, and then it went black.

Air whooshed past Evangeline's face. An engine droned. The odor of dirty dog drifted over from somewhere nearby.

She pried her eyes open.

The night sky was filled with pinpricks of stars rushing by. And of course, there was the full moon, following along above them. They sped past warehouses and docks with the wide, dark Mississippi River flowing beside them. Mrs. Midsomer, still dressed in her satin gown, drove the car. Julian sat in the passenger seat beside his mama. Evangeline herself was squeezed into the center of the tiny convertible's back seat, Gran and Fader to her left and the grim to her right, sitting so tall, he never would have fit if the car's top had been up.

Her eyes closed again.

It was twelve noon. Sunlight streamed through the Midsomers' guest-bedroom window. A knock sounded, the door opened, and Julian entered. Since the rougarou incident a day and a half ago, he'd taken to wearing his own leather satchel strapped across his chest. Evangeline had no idea what he carried inside it, though. Probably superglue and screwdrivers.

"Here's your lunch." He offered her a tray piled with chicken nuggets, carrot sticks, and a can of Coke.

Evangeline's stomach rumbled at the sight and smell. She sat up, wincing as bandages rubbed against wounds, still feeling as though she'd been chewed up and spit out. She propped the pillow behind her, not particularly caring for Julian waiting on her, but she was too hungry to argue.

He set the tray on her lap. "I hope you don't mind I gave your dog a bath. The ASPCA recommends bathing your canine pet at least once every three months. You should always avoid getting water in the ear canals as it can pool there and possibly cause an infection. I stuffed cotton balls in his ears to reduce such a risk."

The grim padded into the room wearing an aroma of mint and coconut, far better than the last time she'd smelled him.

"That calendula salve your gran used on him is working nicely. His wounds are almost completely healed." Julian ruffled the dog's black fur to reveal the encouraging results.

"Thanks." Evangeline shoved a nugget into her mouth. The big dog sat up on his haunches, his yellow eyes fixed intently on her. He licked his lips. She tossed him a nugget, and he caught it and swallowed it whole.

"What are you going to name him?" Julian asked.

"Berus," she said around a mouthful of nugget.

"Berus?"

She swallowed the chicken down with a sip of Coke. "Short for Cerberus. You know, the three-headed hellhound who guards the entrance to the underworld."

Julian regarded the grim for a moment, then gave a crisp nod. "A very suitable moniker."

Gran hobbled up the hallway on a set of crutches and

poked her head into the room, her haunt huntress talisman swaying on its silver chain around her neck. "Percy will be here soon. It's time you stop lounging around like the queen of the Nile and get your things packed up."

"We're going home today?" Evangeline's heart leaped. "But what about the former rougarous and their familiars?"

"Our job is done," Gran replied. "It's up to the law to take it from here."

The thought of returning to the bayou sent a surge of joy coursing through Evangeline's veins. She shoved two more nuggets into her mouth, then scrambled out of bed and grabbed her suitcase.

Two hours and twenty-three minutes later, Percy's rusted red pickup bounced up the street and came to a squealing stop in front of the Midsomers' house. He climbed to the porch, where Gran, Evangeline, and their familiars waited alongside the Midsomer family. After he'd given the proper round of handshakes, hugs, and cheek kisses, he stepped back, set his eyes on Berus, and slid the toothpick from one side of his mouth to the other. "Well, now. Evangeline? You done got yourself a dog?"

"Yep." Evangeline tried not to beam like a fool. "His name's Berus."

Percy reached into the pocket of his sleeveless flannel

shirt, snapped off a big piece of gator jerky, and offered it to the grim. "Hey there, Berus boy." He patted the top of Berus's head with one hand while the big dog licked the gator tidbit from his other.

"And Fader!" Percy crouched to share a morsel with the cat and scratch him between two of his four ears.

Mrs. Midsomer hugged Gran; then she hugged Evangeline. She touched her fingertips to the red gris-gris bag hanging from a cord around her neck. "Thank you. You know you're welcome to come visit anytime."

Mr. Midsomer stepped forward. "Mrs. Holyfield. Evangeline. I wish you would let us pay you something more."

Gran nodded down toward the three bottles of red wine poking out of the top of her valise. "That merlot is payment enough. You just take care of your family. Love them, and never let them go."

Mr. Midsomer put his arms around his wife and his son. "Yes, ma'am. I can promise you that."

"Nice meeting you, Mr. Julian." Gran shook Julian's hand, and as Percy took the suitcases and bags to the truck, she tucked the crutches beneath her arms and made her way down from the porch. Fader scampered after her.

"Well." Evangeline shifted her booted feet, not sure what to say. "I'll be seeing you. Come on, Berus."

She'd made it halfway down the steps when Julian

called out, "Evangeline!"

She turned. "Yeah?"

He hopped down and joined her and Berus on the steps.

Evangeline sniffed and furrowed her brow. "Julian, do you smell like rosemary?"

He nodded. "I hear the aroma brings its wearer good luck." Then he paused for a moment, and his face grew serious. "I'm sorry I doubted you. You were right about everything."

Evangeline flushed with pride, surprised at how much this boy's good opinion of her mattered. "Well, I wasn't right about Camille."

"That's true." He nodded. "I did try to tell you, but you—"

She narrowed her eyes. "Don't push it."

He cleared his throat, then reached into his leather satchel. He pulled out a bowie knife, laid it across his palms, and offered it to her. "To replace the one Laurent broke."

The shiny new blade with the pearl handle shimmered and gleamed in the sunlight. It was the loveliest knife Evangeline had ever set eyes on.

"Thank you." She took it, and after admiring it for a moment longer, she slid it into the leather sheath at her leg, the weight of it somehow making her feel whole again.

She climbed into the truck and took her seat beside

Gran and Fader. Being too big to fit inside the cab with them, Berus had to ride in the back. Evangeline hauled the squealing door shut, then peered out the rear window.

The Midsomer family waved good-bye.

With equal pinches of worry and sadness tugging at her heart, she waved good-bye in return. They were good folk, and she would miss them.

They pulled away from the house, and a white bird soared past the truck. It winged its way up the street and settled onto the shoulder of a tall, gray-bearded man standing within the shadows of a majestic oak on the corner.

As the truck rumbled up the street and past the man, Evangeline gave him a nod, from one professional to another. And Papa Urbain nodded to her in return.

A rush of relief fell over her, and she smiled. There would be no need to worry about the Midsomers now, not with someone here keeping an eye on them.

Percy drove them home, chattering every mile of the way. Evangeline tuned him out. She pressed her fingers to the bandaged wound on her shoulder. With Gran's calendula salve, it would heal, but it would never completely disappear. She knew death's puckered pink mark would remain there, no doubt the first of many scars she'd acquire throughout her life as a haunt huntress. She cast a glance back at the truck's bed and at Berus sitting up tall, the wind ruffling his black fur. She also knew her familiar would remain with her too, no matter where her haunt huntress path might take her.

A week later, the council had not yet convened to decide if Evangeline should be granted her own silver talisman. But she wasn't worried. She didn't need a talisman to prove she was a haunt huntress. Though she had yet to discover what her unique talent would be, she had heart, she had her familiar, and she had some powers. Maybe only a half amount of those powers, but when she needed them, they would be there.

She twisted the lid onto the last jar of fresh aconitum extract she'd prepared that evening. She set the containers in their place on the front-room shelf, then removed her work gloves and gave Berus a pat on his warm, furry head. His tongue lolled, and her heart brimmed with contentment and pride.

Across the room Fader scratched at the front door, yowling to be let out.

"All right." Evangeline pointed a finger of warning at him. "But *no* messenger birds."

Fader fixed his gaze on hers, bent back one set of ears, and twitched his tail.

"Fader . . ." She narrowed her eyes at him.

Fader huffed.

"Good." She opened the door. He scampered out, and true to his name, his dark-gray fur quickly camouflaged him, fading him against the backdrop of the night.

Gran dozed in her rocker there in the front room, one eye open and snoring mightily. Evangeline gave her a kiss on the forehead.

"Come on, Berus. Let's get some sleep." But the command wasn't necessary. The big dog seldom left her side.

She pulled off her boots and climbed into bed, still in her jeans and T-shirt, too exhausted to put on a nightgown. As she drew the old patchwork quilt up to her chin, Berus clambered onto the foot of the bed, causing the springs to creak, and taking up nearly every square inch of available space. He laid his big head on his paws.

Evangeline closed her eyes. She was just drifting to sleep when a tapping sounded against her windowpane.

She peeled her eyelids open. A sparrow perched on the sill, clasping a note in its beak.

She dragged herself out of bed, opened the window, and retrieved the message.

As the bird flapped away into the night, a pair of bright-green eyes watched it from below. She closed the window and unfolded the note. It was addressed to her. She skimmed past Mrs. Arseneau's hastily scrawled message, past the

polite greeting and the customary request for the services of a swamp witch. She ran her eyes farther down the page and finally reached the meat of the matter.

"It's a request to remove a shadow c   her from under the bed," she murmured to Berus. She re   the second-to-last line of Mrs. Arseneau's request: "'Y   have no problem locating the creature, as it smells strongly of smoke, kerosene, and root beer.'" But it was the last line of the note that brought a smile to Evangeline's face and a grumble to her stomach. "'There's also   can pie waiting on the kitchen counter as payment for services.'"

Evangeline folded the note and tucked it into her satchel. She pulled on her priest-blessed, silver-tipped, alligator-skin boots and fastened her pearl-handled bowie knife to her leg.

"Come on, Berus. We're needed."

GLOSSARY
OF MONSTERS, GHOSTS, AND ASSORTED SUPERNATURAL ENTITIES

Acadian fang worm: A fat, round worm roughly three feet long with a tiny, fang-lined mouth that spews venomous acid. Probably a distant relative of the Mongolian death worm that inhabits the most desolate parts of the Gobi Desert in China and Mongolia.

albino channel nixie: A water-dwelling imp with white flesh, white hair, red eyes, and long pink whiskers at the corners of its mouth. It enjoys nipping chunks of flesh from human hands and feet, which it finds much tastier than the insects and crawfish it normally eats in its marshy home.

bayou banshee: A ghostly being with wispy hair, cracked lips, and anguished eyes. Its wails and shrieks can shatter windows. Wearing a spectral gray prison dress, it emerges from its grave at the women's state penitentiary.

blood fae: A tiny, wild gray fairy with shiny black eyes, slits instead of a nose, claws, and sharp teeth. It feeds on blood, and a hungry swarm of them can drain a human body in ten seconds.

cauchemar: A paralyzing nightmare spirit that rides sleeping people like horses, rendering them unable to cry out or move. Sometimes known to even choke or suffocate its victim. It arrived in Louisiana hundreds of years ago when it followed French settlers to the state.

chasse-galerie: A party of ghostly hunters and their dogs. They ride through the night like a fierce wind, bringing with them the sounds of barking, howling, blowing horns, ringing bells, and the shouts of invisible men.

chupacabra: A dark, furry creature with bulging red eyes, fanged teeth, and a row of quills along its back. It stands about four feet tall and walks on two hind legs. A killer of livestock, it drains the blood, leaving behind two puncture marks on its victims' necks.

creeper: A small and harmless spectral being that floats silently after passersby. It is easily dissipated with a swipe of light.

dixie demon: A vicious, shape-shifting being encountered deep in the swamps and woods of Louisiana. First appearing in the form of a harmless person or animal that is distinctly out of place, it will then suddenly sprout a mouthful of sharp teeth and attack its victims.

fifolet: A floating, burning ball of light. Many believe following it will lead to a buried treasure, but it usually only draws people to their doom.

galerie goblin: A short, troublemaking creature with sharp teeth and a nose and ears that are long and pointy. Also known as a porch goblin. Notorious for destabilizing front steps, rocking chairs, and porch columns with the intent of causing injury and embarrassment to humans.

graveyard ghoul: A hunch-shouldered creature with clawed fingers and strong, sinewy arms and legs. Its stringy gray hair resembles Spanish moss, helpful when camouflaging itself among trees. It invades the graves and crypts of the recently deceased and feasts upon their bodies.

greedy grass: A patch of cursed grass that if stepped upon will render its victim suddenly and insatiably hungry, sometimes even causing them to gnaw their own fingers. It emits an aroma the victim perceives as smelling like their favorite food.

grim: A huge, yellow-eyed, shaggy black dog similar in appearance to a Newfoundland. To see one means someone near is about to die. It is fierce, strong, and intelligent and is responsible for escorting the souls of the dead to the other side.

grunch: A creature bearing a set of curved horns but the head, chest, and arms of a man. Its lower body is four-legged and wooly, like that of a ram. It inhabits remote dead-end roads in the undeveloped areas of eastern New Orleans.

hara-hand: An ancient, shriveled, very lively severed human hand, possibly an item of dark magic. Its origin is unknown, only that it was originally found crawling around a festival in Harahan, Louisiana. Thus it acquired the name, the hara-hand.

haunt huntress familiar: An animal distinct in appearance, or at least bearing some unusual markings. It presents itself to its haunt huntress before she reaches her thirteenth birthday. The familiar's particular abilities complement the unique talent of its mistress. Fiercely loyal, it aids and defends its haunt huntress throughout her lifetime, its own life coming to an end within minutes of the death of its mistress. Common examples of haunt huntress familiars include: cats, dogs, hares, hawks, owls, raccoons, rats, and snakes.

hookfoot: A green, tree-dwelling monster with bloodshot eyes, a human-shaped head, powerful jaws, and arrow-shaped teeth. It hangs by its hands from the high branches and snatches up prey with its long mantis-like legs and sharp-taloned feet. It is notorious for toying with its food before devouring it.

hydrangean lizard: A large lizard approximately the length of a medium-sized dog. It possesses the regenerative ability to regrow its lost limbs, tail, and sometimes even its head with multiple replacements. Its diet consists mostly of the flowers of the wild swamp hydrangeas.

Johnny revenant: The reanimated, moldering corpse of a Civil War soldier. It runs through the swamps, crying a shrill rebel yell and using a broken tree limb to wallop anyone in its path.

lootslang: A fanged, snake-like creature about three feet long, covered in bumpy green gator skin and bearing a set of tusks. It camouflages itself in its swampy surroundings and will leave intruders alone unless they began to dig in the area where it resides. It is said to be guarding the buried loot of a pirate.

Mississippi mud man: A big and strong being created from Mississippi River mud for the purpose of performing difficult farm chores.

Nalusa Falaya: A creature that lives in the dense woods near swamps. It is tall and spindly with a shriveled face, small pink eyes, and scaly skin. Though it speaks with a human voice and walks upright, it slides on its stomach like a snake when stalking the victims it will bewitch into doing evil.

rougarou: A wolfman with red eyes, fangs, claws, and brown fur. He walks upright on two bowed legs and is unusually fast and strong. Even though he doesn't feed on blood, he still possesses an overpowering drive to hunt and kill humans. Only the bite of an alpha rougarou can infect a victim, resulting in that victim's transforming into a rougarou on the night of the next full moon.

shadow croucher: A creature that was previously a normal-sized animal but has grown larger and more vicious due to eating poisonous fruit from the tree of fear. Driven by an extreme state of fright, it will attack anyone it encounters. Light repulses it, causing it to hide under beds, in closets, and nearly any place that provides shadow and darkness.

Terrebonne Troll: A burly, bad-tempered, destructive creature nearly seven feet tall. Its skin is pale and pasty, its jaw juts, its brow protrudes, and its huge belly hangs low. Since it never bathes, it also smells bad. It steals food, property, and children—enslaving some of them and attempting to eat the others.

tree of fear: A tree bearing a poisonous fruit that resembles a black, slimy, gassy-smelling plum. Any creature eating the fruit will transform into a fear-filled shadow croucher.

yimmby: A gray-skinned being less than eight inches tall. It has a potbelly, two thin legs, long feet, round eyes, and wiry white hairs on its head. It loves to eat and will consume large amounts of food that it steals from humans.

ACKNOWLEDGMENTS

My heartfelt thanks to my husband, Charlie, for his steadfast love and support, and to my kids, Jamie, Chase, and Savannah—sorry for ignoring you guys all those times I was writing, and extra thanks to Chase for his fantastic brainstorming ideas.

My wholehearted thanks to the publishing rock stars who believed in me: Elena Giovinazzo—the best agent ever; the wonderful Holly McGhee; the brilliant Alessandra Balzer; and the delightfully imaginative Joseph Kuefler.

My hearty thanks to my extraordinary beta readers: Amy Paulshock, Marcea Ustler, and Ann Meier, and to my other extraordinary critique group members: Taryn Souders, Leslie Santa Maria, Ruth Owen, Charlotte Hunter, Brian Crawford, Lynne Ryder, and Kimberly Lekman. And also to Ed Masessa and Zebo Ludvicek for just being awesome; Linda Rodriguez Bernfeld, our hardworking FL SCBWI regional advisor; and all my other writing-family members for their friendship and encouragement over the years: Lisa Iriarte, Joe Iriarte, Jennye Kamin, Alina Blanco, Mark Chick, Brian Truitt, Usman Malik, Charles Waters, Marlana Antifit, Rina Heisel, Peggy Jackson, Vivi Barnes, Dennis Cooper, Stephanie Spier, and Barb Nefer.

JAN ELDREDGE was born and raised in Louisiana. She now lives in Florida with her husband, their children, and a house full of cats. When she's not writing, she spends her time reading, going to theme parks, and exploring old cemeteries. She is particularly fascinated with monsters, magic, and all such eldritch things. You can visit her online at www.JanEldredge.com.

JOSEPH KUEFLER is the author-illustrator of *Beyond the Pond*, *Rulers of the Playground*, and *The Digger and the Flower*. He lives in Minnesota with his wife and children. You can visit him online at www.josephkuefler.com.